c.3

Hamilton
  The last shot.

DATE DUE

THE LAST
SHOT

THE LAST SHOT

SHOT

Hugo Hamilton

Farrar Straus Giroux

NEW YORK

C. 3

Copyright © 1991 by Hugo Hamilton
All rights reserved
First published in 1991 by Faber & Faber Limited, London
First American edition, 1992
Printed in the United States of America

Library of Congress Cataloging-in-Publication Data
Hamilton, Hugo.
The last shot / Hugo Hamilton.—1st American ed.
p. cm.
I. Title.
PR6058.A5526L37   1992   823'.914—dc20   91-40280   CIP

für Irmgard

THE LAST
SHOT

An American man, born of a doomed love
affair at the end of World War II, re-
turns to Czechoslovakia and Germany in
the 1980's to search for his father.

1

At 7.15 a.m. Bertha Sommer walked down the road from the main German garrison towards the town of Laun. She was on her way to the church of St Nicholas, where she would attend Mass, something she was determined not to miss no matter what events would take place on that day. 'No matter how close the Russians are,' she said to herself defiantly. It was a clear May morning: May 1945. The relentless rain of the night before had stopped, and even though banks of cloud still hung over the eastern sky, there was a feeling that the weather would change. An intuition of summer.

She was accompanied by an officer named Franz Kern whose noisy boots sometimes obscured the sound of her own footsteps. He was with her for her own protection. Her escort. The roads of Bohemia were no longer safe. And as they walked down the hill, the town of Laun was frozen below them in a patient immobility, blue woodsmoke rising above the roofs in the distance like a symbol of static hostility. The Czechs knew their day of freedom would come soon, but the feeling was tinged with the innate provincial fear which has clung to this small town ever since; the fear of being left behind by history. Time moves on, towns don't.

The road was loud with birdsong. There was little to talk about as they walked. Bertha Sommer knew Officer Kern from the office where they saw each other regularly, though they seldom talked about anything other than official matters. Outside the office, there was nothing to say. In May 1945 there was so much on everybody's mind. So much you couldn't talk about. Or maybe it was the sheer volume of things to say that forced them instead to speak about nothing but the rain.

'It kept me awake,' she said openly. 'I thought it would never end.'

Bertha was sure she had already said too much. It was followed by the silence along the road; their footsteps, the hysterical noise of birds and, somewhere in the distance, the familiar hoarse bark of a dog she had often heard before at this point on the road, but never actually seen. The rain had unleashed the fresh damp smell of the soil. It merged with the smell of exhaust left behind by military trucks.

In the small Bohemian town of Laun, where this story begins, somewhere almost halfway between Prague and Dresden, it was impossible to pretend that everything went on as normal. Europe was in ruins. Hitler was dead. There wasn't much left of Dresden. The smell of Russian cigarettes came from the east, where the Red Army stood somewhere between Brno and Jihlava, advancing at a rate of eighty kilometres per day. The smell of Camel cigarettes was even closer, drifting up from Pilsen in the south, where the Americans had stopped, having consented by nodding agreement that the liberation of Czechoslovakia belonged to the Russians. It was a matter of waiting. The radio stations coming from Dresden and from Prague went on broadcasting German march music. Occasionally you heard German swing. Mostly it was waltz music. The Reich was waltzing to an end.

The resistance movement in Czechoslovakia had planned their nationwide insurrection for that day. Everything was set for the liberation of Prague, the only European capital left under occupation. But the Reich held fast. There was talk of fighting to the last man. Orders were given by General Schörner in command of the German Army on the Eastern Front that any German soldier caught deserting or attempting to flee should be hanged on the spot. They were already dangling from the trees elsewhere, in Prussia. In defeat, the army hangs its own.

What everybody really wanted was to go home. The whole of Europe was thinking about home, or what was left of it. Bertha Sommer thought about Kempen, a small town no larger than Laun, but over 1,000 kilometres to the west, in the Rhineland. Officer Kern thought about Nuremberg, or what was left of it.

Going home wasn't that simple. Not so easy to end a war. A war is only over when the last shot has been fired, and who knows where the last shot of the Second World War was fired?

Back in April, when all German civilians were finally allowed to evacuate from the Czech protectorate back to German soil, the commander of the garrison at Laun issued a directive confining the remaining civilian backup personnel to barracks for their own safety. It could only have been intended for one person. Bertha Sommer. She was the last person left at the garrison of 2,000 infantry men of the 213th Battalion who could be described under this directive. She began to plead with Hauptmann Selders to be exempted. She was determined to go to Mass throughout the month of May. It was that important to her. Hauptmann Selders said he would hate to lose his last secretarial assistant to a partisan bullet along the open roads. But he was flexible and eventually changed the directive. From now on, he decreed that civilian backup personnel had to travel in armoured cars, until he reflected on the fuel shortages and changed his mind again; they had to be accompanied by an armed soldier. He put it in writing. She typed it up. Officer Franz Kern volunteered.

Bertha Sommer wore a three-quarter-length russet coat. In the early morning light along the road down to Laun, Officer Kern would have thought the colour of the coat leaned more towards burgundy or wine. But the exact colour of her coat had always been a matter of some dispute, ever since she bought it in Paris. Her own mother called it copper. The inhabitants of Laun, who were convinced that she was sent to the St Nicholas church to spy on them, said the coat was fox-red, or fox-brown.

Bertha Sommer walked briskly. Perhaps it was her shyness. She began to count her own footsteps. She idly measured the distance to the next building in footsteps; the first small house on the outskirts of the town.

'Fräulein Sommer.' Officer Kern addressed her quite abruptly. 'Do you realize how close we are to the end?'

'What do you mean?' She was trying to read the implication.

'It's over. The Reich is finished. You have seen all the reports. It may not even last the day. Do you realize what this means for you?'

'Yes and no.'

Occasionally their footsteps fell into unison, causing a slight embarrassment between them until her faster steps doubled his once more.

'Fräulein Sommer, have you any idea how close we are to Russian captivity? For your sake, Fräulein Sommer, I would avoid this at all cost. Above all people, I would hate to see you taken into Russian hands.'

'What are you suggesting?' she said.

There was another moment of raw embarrassment. He apologized for putting it so crudely but he felt he had to warn her. Even then, his open discussion of German defeat was enough to condemn him for treason. Enough to have him shot or hanged from the next tree. Now she began to wonder why he had volunteered to walk down to the town with her. His honesty scared her. She suspected it was a trick. Something to test her loyalty. You could trust nobody in the Reich. And yet, he was only saying what everyone had felt privately for months.

'Between the two of us, Fräulein Sommer, I think we should get out of Laun as soon as possible. Things are going to get very bad around here. I may be able to arrange something, so I would ask you to be prepared. The sooner we set off back towards Eger, to the German border, the better.'

'Herr Kern, are you talking about desertion?'

'Fräulein Sommer, I wish you wouldn't put it like that. You are a civilian in the service of the Wehrmacht, how can you desert? There is no point in your being here with the army to the bitter end.

'And it's going to be bitter, believe me. I hear everything that's going on. It's my job to listen to all radio signals. I know what's going to happen here when the Russians arrive. Very briefly, Fräulein Sommer, I have a simple plan to get you back to Germany. I may be able to arrange it tonight. Think about it.

4

Don't give me an answer now. Let it go through your head. But whatever happens, I would advise you to be ready to leave at a moment's notice.'

Bertha said nothing. She kept walking as though she could pretend at any moment to have heard nothing. Why was this officer so interested in her welfare? She searched for motives. Gave no hint of collusion. She listened.

'This may be your last chance to get back to Germany. The people in our garrison may never see their homes again . . .' Officer Kern hesitated. 'I want to offer you that chance, at least.'

When Officer Kern unexpectedly looked into her eyes she may have unconsciously given him some encouragement, because he began to unveil his plan as they walked.

'At eleven o'clock this evening,' he said, 'you will see a Lazarett vehicle marked with the Red Cross by the main gates. It's there every night. If you're sitting in that truck by half-eleven, you're with us. There are three of us. There is room for one more. Bring only one light bag and don't let anyone see you.'

She acknowledged nothing and gave no indication whether she would be there or not. She felt that Officer Kern had shown her enormous trust. An almost indecent trust. She could have gone straight back and reported the plan, though it would be unlike her to do so. But she was afraid that she had already been dragged into a conspiracy by his talk. The fact that such an offer was put to her would force her to consider it. One way or the other, she would have to answer.

He told her to think it over. It was up to her. He would not be offended if she ignored it.

'Just remember, Fräulein Sommer, when the Russians get to Laun, we can expect very little sympathy from them, or the Czechs. You know what's happened around these parts. They'll all be hungry for revenge. All these Sudeten Germans will be for it.'

She thought she knew what he was referring to. The occupation of Czechoslovakia. She knew nothing more. She knew nothing of Theresienstadt, forty kilometres east of Laun along

5

the same river. She could imagine nothing like it. She walked into the church. Officer Kern held the large oak door open for her, nodded and stepped back outside, where he waited for her to pray and make up her mind. He was Lutheran. He stood at the bottom of the steps outside.

Inside, Bertha Sommer kneeled once again before the massive wooden carving which covered the end wall of the church behind the altar. The interior of the church had become so familiar to her over the months she had spent in Laun that her opinions began to repeat themselves. The great wood carving seemed a little out of place for this small church; it belonged more to a cathedral. The May altar for Our Lady was decorated with extra flowers. She tried to keep her mind on the Mass. She tried to put everything secular out of her head.

If you want to know what Bertha Sommer did during the Second World War: she prayed. That morning, though, she could hardly concentrate. Nothing could keep out the fragile reality of her situation in Laun. She kept wondering whether she would ever see her home again; her mother, her sisters, her aunt, her home town of Kempen. Struck by a sudden impatience, she wanted to go home that minute, and involuntarily she began to weigh up Officer Kern's plan for escape.

Bertha prayed for guidance. She expected somehow to be given a divine signal. During the course of Mass she changed her mind at least a half-dozen times. She could not come to terms with the idea of desertion. It was dishonest, and dangerous. She kept thinking about Officer Kern's subversive proposal. Could she trust him, she wondered. She had nobody to talk to about it but God. She would let God decide.

2

The barber's shop on Prag Strasse in Laun was busy that morning. It could have been taken for some kind of symbol or national expression of independence that men arrived early to get their hair cut. Apart from Mass at the church of St Nicholas, it was the only good excuse any man could invent to be seen so early. The horizontal blinds of this front-room barber's shop gave an excellent view on to the main street, on to the pub across the road and everything that moved through the town.

There was a group of men waiting to have their hair cut, four men and a small Down's Syndrome boy who stood by the window. They all had seen the new armoured patrol arrive to replace the night patrol on the square. And the German woman on foot, in her red coat, along with a German officer.

The men sat along a wooden bench and said nothing. They felt the silent, reflective moment that all men feel before their turn comes up in the barber's chair, the moment preceding change. From time to time they found something to whisper about. Occasionally the barber joined in with a discreet word in somebody's ear as he drew the sheet up and stuffed it into the collar of his next customer. But the clicking of scissors took over and covered everything with a feverish whisper of its own.

The boy with Down's Syndrome clapped when his father settled into the barber's chair. He ran back and forth to the window, excited about everything, occasionally receiving a smile of acknowledgement from the men along the bench. He had red hair. Saliva ran down to his chin and there was a damp stain on his chest where it collected. He was no more than four years of age. Born during the war. The very existence of a boy with Down's Syndrome was an overt act of revolution in the Reich.

The Czech liberation came late. They could have waited for the Russians but they were anxious to strike a blow for independence. A home-made revolution.

Throughout April the resistance movement had obstructed German military movement by bombing railways, disabling locomotives, tanks, armoured units and generally supporting the Russian advance. The aim was to be a nuisance. They blew up fuel reserves, and when the German Army resorted to using alcohol to power their vehicles, the Czechs began to spill bottles and barrels of schnapps and slivovitz into the streets; bottles they would soon need to celebrate victory when they were eventually liberated.

The men in Laun were waiting for the signal. They were already aware that on the previous day men from the nearby mining town of Kladno had marched to Hriskov, south of Laun, with no more than a ration of cigarettes in their pockets, to take over the German arms dump there. The Czechs needed weapons. In Prague, they planned to fight with furniture. With barricades. In another north Bohemian town, the people tried to do without weapons altogether and came out on the streets for a peaceful protest, a premature but unsuccessful attempt at the velvet approach. General Schörner told his troops 'to quell any such disturbances with the most ruthless force'.

The men at the barber's shop in Laun were waiting for the right moment to assemble and form a National Committee of independent Czechoslovakia. All they needed was a leader. They sat watching the boy with Down's Syndrome playing with the cords of the blinds by the window. The boy groaned in a world of his own. Occasionally, he turned around and addressed one of the men without the slightest hint of shyness, his upper lip drawn up toward his nose, genetically disfigured into a permanent smile.

'Who's next?' the barber asked, knowing that a son follows after a father.

The boy sat down on his father's knee and allowed the barber to hang a sheet around him and tuck it under the collar. It was

8

all new to him. He was silent, reassured by his father's words, until the barber began to clip rhythmically with the scissors. 'There's a good boy,' the barber kept saying. But even before the scissors had touched the boy's hair, he began to struggle and make life difficult. The white sheet had already come undone. There was no point in putting it back. Instead, the barber manoeuvred himself around the chair as best he could to try and get at the boy's hair.

Both the father and the barber tried to distract the boy. 'Look, look in the mirror. Look, there's a good boy.' The barber tapped the mirror with his scissors. 'There's a good boy. Nearly finished,' he kept saying.

But the boy soon began to wail. Not so much like crying, but a solid howl; half fear and half mistrust. He kept looking around to see what was going on but he couldn't understand the purpose of the scissors. He tried to free his arms from his father's grip. Wisps of cut hair fell into his eyes, tickled his nose and his neck behind his collar. Nobody could explain it to him. The barber got a scented towel and wiped it over the boy's face, taking away a mixture of saliva, cut hair and tears.

Another armoured car went by outside. The barber managed to deflect the boy's attention for long enough to clip a semi-circle over the ears. The fingers of his left hand pinned the boy's head down vigorously. But the sound of the scissors magnified in the boy's ears to the size of shears and he resumed his howls, louder than ever.

The whole barber's shop had become occupied with the boy's haircut. Once again the barber made an attempt to distract the boy. He took out two ivory brushes, clacked them together and gave them to the boy. The barber rushed around, exploiting the moment. It was a race against time, before the boy dropped the brushes again and put his hands up. That was enough. His father released him and the boy jumped down, running into the centre of the room.

'Vla, vla,' he said, holding his ears, showing off his haircut to the men waiting on the bench.

9

That was the morning the Czechs finally decided to liberate themselves from the fascists and hand themselves over to the communists. The grand uprising in Prague had begun. The whole country was rising up in support. In Laun, a man named Jaroslav Süssmerlich walked into the pub U Somolu at 81 Prag Strasse and convened the first meeting of the National Committee. The men at the barber's shop abandoned their places in the queue and joined him.

They demanded the immediate surrender. They wanted nothing but outright capitulation. By phone, Jaroslav Süssmerlich translated the anger of the town and told the Germans they were ready to attack the garrison. The men from Kladno had already taken the arms dump at Hriskov. But the German commander in Laun made it clear that he had no authority to capitulate until orders came from Prague; from the German High Command. Besides, they held a number of key prisoners; Czech resistance fighters. It became a hostage drama. Negotiations became a race against time. Nobody realized that the Russians were approaching from the north instead of the south.

3

Bertha Sommer emerged from the church of St Nicholas, pushing the heavy oak door like a child. The idea of heavy oak doors in churches is to make people feel small and innocent; children of God. She adjusted her hat, blessed herself from the font and looked down the steep concrete steps, where she saw an armoured car parked along the kerb. It was the only vehicle in the street. The engine was running. Officer Kern stood beside the driver and both of them looked up at her. There was something wrong. She knew it.

Around her, everything else in the street bore the inertia of centuries. The houses, the dusty windows, the grey roofs, all looked as though they would never change.

Bertha Sommer had a good nose. It was the way Officer Kern looked at her as she descended the church steps that told her something had changed. For a moment, she thought she was being arrested for betrayal of the Reich. Either that, or she was fleeing straight away, back to the German border. She told herself she didn't care. After the initial fright, there is always a moment of indifference.

She smelled a wisp of woodsmoke drifting down the street. Nothing visible, beyond the faint blue tint in the distance above the houses. It was a reassurance. Bertha knew every kind of smoke. She had smelled all the different smokes of the war: gunsmoke, fires, scorched landscape, phosphor smoke; even the smell of burning hair. She feared and respected every smell. She then got the smell of Officer Kern's cigarette.

Kern looked serious. When he spoke to her, it was back to his official voice. The former intimacy was ignored. She expected the worst.

'Fräulein Sommer, we have instructions to return to the

garrison immediately. By right, I should have conveyed this to you without delay. We must go straight away.'

He held the door of the vehicle for her and whispered, as she held her hat to get in, 'There's nothing to worry about.'

Afterwards, she felt foolish to have mistrusted him so much. She felt naïve, and envied the way men always seemed to know everything first. Inside the church, she had been under the brief illusion that it was raining outside, only to come out and find the street dry and the sun trying to break through the clouds at last.

The driver turned the vehicle and headed back through the town, past the square, along the main street towards the hill leading up to the garrison.

'Apparently there is something going on here in the town,' Kern said to her in the back of the car. 'Hauptmann Selders has ordered all personnel off the streets.'

Kern didn't discuss it any more. She asked him what it meant but he put a finger over his lips and pointed at the silent driver. They all went mute and looked out of the windows. Bertha saw nothing. No sign of anything going on. At the end of the town, she spotted two women hanging out washing. On a wall, she saw a ginger-coloured cat preparing to jump down. Smoke rose from the last three chimneys in the town. Nothing would ever change the speed of smoke rising from a chimney on a calm day in May.

Her own life would soon accelerate beyond recognition. After months and months of waiting, since Christmas, she would finally move into a new, though perhaps uncertain future. Anything was better than waiting. She thought of Caen in Normandy where she had spent most of the war. And the trips to Paris which had been so exciting. Czechoslovakia had provided none of that excitement. It became the place to wait for the war to end. She could only think of home. She could only think of the frustrating irony that the car in which she sat was actually travelling in the wrong direction. East. Into the arms of the Russians.

She turned around to look through the back window at the town. It may be the last look, she thought. Everywhere Bertha Sommer went, she called things by a private, arcane name in her own mind. As the armoured car climbed the hill back towards the garrison, she looked back and called it: the hill of the last time looking back. The morning of the end of the Reich, she said to herself as they drove through the gates.

'Tonight,' Officer Kern whispered discreetly to her as she got out of the car. She didn't respond. She watched him click his heels and bow slightly, before he marched away towards the command centre.

4

I always thought it was strange that things between Anke and myself ended with a crash. Or was that actually the beginning? It was in Jürgen's car. Just coming off the *Autobahn*, heading back into the centre of Düsseldorf, we were hit by another car. Don't ask me how. All I know is that I'm certain it wasn't my fault. The other car came out of a slip road and hit us on Anke's side, the passenger side. It was in the evening. Dark. Wet. Autumn. I only remember the bang and the sudden immobility afterwards. It was like being attacked for no reason. Neither Anke nor I suffered any real injuries. It all must have looked much worse than it was because the other car had been over-turned by the impact. I thought the occupants must be dead, because nobody moved. But it turned out that the driver, a middle-aged woman, escaped gracefully with nothing more than concussion.

The big problem was that I was driving. I was sitting in the driving seat of Jürgen's car. A car I wasn't insured to drive and a car I shouldn't have been sitting in at all in the first place. Anke was hurt. The other car had crashed into us from the right and Anke had got a terrible thump all the way down from her shoulder to her knee. Even though nothing was broken, she was badly bruised.

'I'm all right, I'm all right,' she kept saying, hysterically reassuring herself, or both of us. 'It's nothing. Honestly.'

All we thought of at that moment was the fact that I was in the driving seat. Uninsured. Without a licence to drive in Germany. The complications would have been enormous. Like all sur-vivors, glad to be alive and uninjured, we reassured ourselves that nothing else mattered. But then, when we saw that the street was empty and that nobody had emerged from the overturned car, we thought again. We could get away with it.

'Quick,' Anke said, hauling herself up out of the seat. 'Quick, before the police arrive.'

She manoeuvred herself across me as best she could. A swift seat-change inside the car. Once she was in the driving seat and I was in the passenger seat, everything seemed all right. At least we could explain that much. It was only when she sat back with the steering wheel in her hands that she said she began to feel any pain at all on her right side.

I can never be sure if Jürgen ever discovered that I was driving. Or if he ever found out where Anke and I could have been to in his car. Or what we were up to. Anke was already married to Jürgen. Just married, in fact. I had been at the wedding not long before that.

The idea of Anke and I driving off together like this was her strange notion of a final farewell; Anke's idea of saying goodbye to me, taking me back to the Eifel mountains, to the exact spot where we went the first time. She was basically meeting me for the last time as a lover, a formal rite whereby she was now ceremoniously entering into a new life with Jürgen. From now on she would be married. Why she left this intimate farewell until a month after the wedding was beyond me. I have never fully understood Anke.

The crash must have changed her plans. It placed us together in a further conspiracy. Because we had switched places inside the car, we were bound together for ever in a fraud. We were going to have to tell lies. And then back-up lies with more lies. We were going to have to discuss and plan out a communal approach.

We didn't know what to tell Jürgen. How was I going to explain being in the car in the first place? Even as we sat in the car, shocked, waiting for the police or an ambulance or something, Anke suggested that I should just walk away, pretend that she was the only occupant in the car. There was nobody around. It might have worked. But I was against it, instinctively. I stayed.

Walking away never works. I began to think about the driver of the other car, overturned, right behind us. I had difficulty opening the door on my side, but I got out and went over to see. I told Anke to stay in the driver's seat. Eventually, people came out from houses near by and called an ambulance. The woman in the other car was unconscious, though when she was taken away one of the ambulance men said she would be fine. Anke was taken to hospital too, for observation, overnight.

It was up to me to phone and tell Jürgen. And somehow, maybe because Jürgen and I have known each other for so long, there was no immediate pressure for an explanation. All Jürgen wanted to know was that she was all right. What hospital? What ward? He didn't ask me how I knew or how it happened or anything. I volunteered nothing.

In the end, I left it to Anke to do all the talking, since the whole thing was her idea in the first place. When Jürgen arrived at the hospital that night he still wasn't asking for an explanation, and Anke said little else other than that she had been giving me a lift home. We had met for a drink. The fact that the location of the crash didn't correspond with my route home from anywhere never came up. Nor did the fact that her injuries were on the wrong side of her body.

I went to visit her at the hospital early the next day, before she was discharged, to see what she had said to Jürgen. She showed me her bruises. She didn't remember being hit at all. But the proof was there. A massive blue, black, purple cloud under her swollen skin, all along her arm, and down the side of her right thigh. There was a small bandage on her thigh where the skin had burst.

'Looks lovely, doesn't it?' she said. 'I've got myself a fine-looking mark there.'

'Does it hurt?' I asked.

'Not in the least,' she said. 'I'm quite proud of it. The only thing that bothers me are these endless X-rays.'

She pulled back the sheet and showed me the full extent of

the bruising. Everybody has a natural fascination for injuries. You want to see more.

'Do you want to kiss my bruise?' she asked.

I ignored her because it made me uneasy. I knew that Jürgen was coming to collect her any minute. She stuck her tongue out at me and covered herself up again. That was Anke all right. She was always sticking her tongue out like that.

'What are you going to say to Jürgen?' I asked.

'Nothing. I'll tell him everything. The whole thing, if he asks.'

'Everything?'

'Well, the only thing he doesn't need to know is that you were driving his car. I think we should keep that a secret for the moment.'

Jürgen never asked. There was never anything said about the crash. I think Jürgen was glad that nothing worse had happened to Anke. No broken bones. He was concerned for her. He also asked how I was. Maybe it was his medical background, his doctor's instinct for discretion.

The fact that Jürgen never pursued any questions made me think even more. I slowly began to believe that it was Jürgen who had sent Anke on this farewell trip with me. Maybe they did have a pact. Maybe he had some notion that one final trip up to the Eifel would end it for Anke and me. One last goodbye to a past lover. And the fact that Jürgen, a doctor, a highly intelligent man with an inquiring mind, never noticed that the bruises were on the wrong side worried me. But then, nobody else asked either.

We let the lies stand.

5

Before Bertha Sommer reported for work that morning she went to her room to pack. She was taking Officer Kern's advice and decided to have a light bag ready so she could leave at a moment's notice. She had made no final decision about fleeing that evening; she was still tormenting herself with the choice. Desert, or stay and face the Russians. One way or the other, she wanted to be ready.

She made two selections of clothes; an A selection and a B selection. Clothes she wanted to take with her and those she would simply have to leave behind. Occasionally she would hold up a garment, like the pale blue blouse, remembering the shop in Paris where she had bought it, and then transfer it from the B selection back to the A selection.

She thought about Officer Kern. He had an honest face. A face she could trust. She knew he was married. He had told her that quite openly when they first met in the office in January. He told her then that there was a lady's bicycle belonging to his wife Monica left behind in the garrison. He and his wife used to go cycling together in the summer. Fräulein Sommer was welcome to make use of the bike any time she wanted. But the weather in January was too cold for cycling. And when the spring came, the environs of Laun became too dangerous. Besides, then came the directive from Hauptmann Selders, confining everyone to the garrison.

Officer Kern was a calm man. He seemed to know everything. He was a man of predictions. Even back in January he had told her the war wouldn't last long. And when the war was over, the bicycle would become the fastest mode of transport in the whole of Europe. He would be sorry to leave it behind.

He had a married look about him, she thought, as she sorted

her clothes. She packed her bag with her sisters in mind. Then she took everything out again and packed it more sensibly, thinking of the worst. She laid out her russet coat and hat on the bed. It was time to go to the office.

She had gone through all this before, evacuating back from Caen in Normandy, running from the British. Now she was running from something worse. She kneeled down and prayed, silently. She was ready for God. Then she quickly wrote a note in her diary, which lay on the table. The morning of the end of the Reich. Packed my bags. Am I a civilian? How will they treat civilians?

Bertha Sommer spent the morning trying to get through to Berlin. She knew it was useless but she kept trying. Berlin was well lost by now. The Russian flag had flown from the roof of the *Reichstag* since 30 April. Another officer kept trying to get through to Prague, with no more success. The office had worked itself into a quiet panic. Cups of coffee were frequently started but seldom finished. Hauptmann Selders fought off the constant demands of the Czechs in Laun. He had already made the concession of withdrawing the army from the town. He fought off the almost hourly demands to surrender with the single remaining advantage left to him. In the end, he could bargain with hostages. But there was no question of capitulation or further withdrawal until he got word from the High Command.

Bertha didn't see Officer Kern anywhere. She knew where he was, in the communications room next door, but she wondered why he hadn't been seen in the office.

By mid-morning she had become so busy herself that she forgot everything. She had been asked to sort out the files on to a trolley. Ready for incineration. Lunchtime passed without anybody getting hungry. Hauptmann Selders ordered a Wurst sandwich but never touched it when it arrived. The other officers had no appetite either. And when Bertha went to the canteen, she had to force herself to have lunch, telling herself it might be the last. But the logic was no substitute for appetite.

She was thinking too much. She had been put in charge of erasing the records. How to end a war? We know how to start a war, she thought. We know nothing about finishing it.

Early afternoon, Officer Kern came rushing into the office for the first time. He had heard something. At 1.30, the radio signal from Prague was interrupted. A spokesman in Czech appealed to all factions throughout Czechoslovakia to rise up against the fascists. Minutes later the Germans had regained control of the station. But it had become obvious that there was a struggle on for the capital. It became clear why they had also lost contact with Prague on the phone.

Hauptmann Selders called his officers for an impromptu conference. Another phone-call came from the town demanding immediate capitulation.

Everyone looked at Hauptmann Selders, waiting for him to announce withdrawal. He made a brief speech. Bertha Sommer stopped sorting files to listen. But her heart sank. She had expected something else.

'There remains only one option open to us at present,' he said. 'While the German Army is still at war, we must remain firm. We cannot act in our own self-interest and make an escape bid. To do so would be irresponsible and put at risk thousands of German civilians still on Czech soil. We would also put ourselves at risk. You know the terms under which General Schörner operates. We must wait for the command.'

Bertha thought for a moment that he was referring to her. To Officer Kern's escape plan. She looked at him standing by the window, but he didn't look back. She felt implicated, even though she had consented to nothing.

'At the same time,' Hauptmann Selders said, 'we should be ready to move out immediately.'

The officers agreed with Hauptmann Selders's decision. There was no dissent. Arrangements were being made for the inevitable evacuation. One officer put forward a plan to use the hostages. Everybody went back to work.

Bertha spent the afternoon burning. A large punctured fuel

bin had been placed in the centre of the square outside on her instructions. She had been told to oversee the burning personally.

The afternoon turned out bright and sunny. Looking south, she saw beams of sunlight lancing through the clouds on to the rounded hills. It looked as though the rain would hold off for a while. She didn't need her coat.

She accompanied two recruits to the store-room on the far side of the square where a consignment of fuel was kept for the sole purpose of destroying documents. She had stacked most of the files on to two trolleys. Two more recruits came out pushing the trolleys into the square. There was nothing of great importance in the files, nothing but reports on resistance operations, command structures and details of the garrison's personnel, names, ranks etc. She was told to burn everything. All over Germany, she thought, people are burning the past.

She placed some of the documents into the bin and stood back. One of the recruits stepped forward and poured some fuel over the documents. It was all done systematically, without any sense of urgency, or regret.

Bertha looked in the direction of the garrison's main gates. Her mind was on escape.

Taking account of the wind direction, one of the soldiers politely advised her to stand back where the smoke would not contaminate her clothes. She saw him strike the match, an act that was no different to clicking his fingers. It was the first time she fully understood the qualities of petrol, a silent blast of flames sucking air violently from the surrounding space, from around her ears and her face.

One by one, she handed the documents over to the soldiers, who added them to the pyre. This was the way to end a war. Without a word. Bertha did ask one of them what area of Germany he came from: Dortmund. But it led to nothing. They went silently about the task, preparing for withdrawal. Later on, Hauptmann Selders came out carrying a number of files which he added to the fire himself. He stood with her for a moment until he saw his own documents disappear. Throughout the afternoon, the flames were reflected in their eyes, in the windows of surrounding buildings and across the windscreens of trucks on the far side of the square.

By late afternoon, the clouds had taken over the sky once more. When the flames receded the charred remnants of paper began to curl and crinkle as they shrank. It doesn't take long to burn a garrison with three companies of Ersatz Grenadiers of the 213th Battalion out of existence.

6

That was typical Anke, sticking out her tongue. For her it was really an expression of affection. Maybe with a bit of daring and natural contempt thrown in. She was into expressions. It was one of the things that struck me most about Anke when I met her first, at the university.

I told her she had jumped the queue in the *Mensa*. She stuck her tongue out at me.

I had been living in Düsseldorf for a number of years at that stage. Why Düsseldorf, I don't really know. I could have stayed in Vermont, where I come from, or chosen any other city in America for a good clean American education. There is something about Germany that I want. Something that everybody secretly wants and openly denies. I opted for a European education at the university in Düsseldorf, where I studied German classics.

Jürgen was studying medicine there at the time. Later, he went on to do gynaecology. But while he was a student, we became good friends. In those five or six years, long before Anke came on the scene, Jürgen and I went everywhere together: Morocco, Greece, Peru, Ireland. He was a perfect travelling partner and a perfect friend. We always knew when to leave each other alone and when to be there to pick each other up. Some of those mornings after the Irish bars I was glad to have a doctor friend. With time, though, Jürgen's job became more demanding. He grew a moustache and we travelled less together. He once took a two-week job in Baghdad during the Iran–Iraq war, and I wasn't able to go. I think that was the first time he went anywhere without me.

We stayed the best of friends. Maybe the only real friends either of us ever had. Mutually exclusive. I think Jürgen would agree with that in theory. We never stopped being friends.

But then came Anke. Anke Seidel.

Everything changed after she arrived. She was wilder than Jürgen and myself put together. There was no time for moderation or discretion. She kept saying there was no such thing as an afterlife. The day after she stuck her tongue out at me, she invited me for a drive to the Eifel mountain range. With her mother's car, a case of her father's champagne and a small Bavarian snuffbox full of cocaine, she drove the Audi into the Eifel in the middle of March. She showed me some of the landmarks, like Camp Vogelsang where Hitler trained his elite young successors. As promised, she also showed me where Heinrich Böll used to live. He was a hero. He had taught her how to cry.

That was the other thing about Anke. She was able to cry. She had a spiritual side to her. She could cry at will. In the car, she told me straight off that she had practised it when she was a child. She and her sister used to look in the mirror and summon up the emotion until the tears ran down. They once sat in the back of the car crying while their parents went shopping, and passers-by began to look into the car and worry about them until they burst out laughing. Her mother berated her for playing with her emotions. Never play with your sacred, involuntary faculties.

I didn't believe that Anke could cry on the spot. Like a movie star. We had a long conversation about it as she drove the car. Then she stopped the car and started crying. Okay, it was outside Heinrich Böll's house, but still and all, she did it. I was moved. So much so that I told her to stop crying.

It's what she said afterwards that worried me. It sounded as though she was clocking up all her crying in advance. Advent-tears.

'Maybe some day, I'll have something to cry about,' she said, laughing, as she drove on.

'I'll give you something to cry about,' I said, as a joke.

I was never any good at jokes. I always listen too much to the prediction of words. We dropped the subject and drove on into the mountains.

Eventually she stopped the car at a remote forest for a picnic. She got me to open the champagne and then dealt out a line of coke on the dashboard of her mother's car, which we snorted with a 100 DM note. Ten minutes later, she handed me her glass to hold for a minute before she opened the door of the car and stepped outside. She leaned back in and said: 'If you can catch me, you can have me.' Then she slapped her bottom and ran off into the trees.

I believe she let me catch her.

It burned intensely for a short while between Anke and myself. We were seen everywhere together. But then, after about two months, she took an equally sudden, but even stronger liking to Jürgen. It seemed far more durable between them right from the beginning. In fact, he seemed to settle her down quite a bit. From time to time, she did revert to me, briefly, for an afternoon, a night, a weekend at most. But she was already leaning more and more towards Jürgen. Then she moved in with him altogether. In less than a year, they decided to get married, which they did with a great carnival in August of 1984. I was left trying to work out what it was that Jürgen had and I didn't. It was more than the moustache.

Then came the crash. Anke and I drove up to the Eifel for the last time. To what she called the consecrated forest. You can see why I was beginning to think that Jürgen was in on it as well; as though he had made a deal with her. But then I realized it was much more like one of her own plans. Anke's farewell.

Since the crash I have been back home to Vermont, wondering if I should leave Germany to Jürgen and Anke. I really thought that in order to forget Anke, I would literally have to leave the country. We were still the best of friends, all of us, and we kept on meeting. They went on inviting me to dinner parties along with other friends. Occasionally I met them for drinks at the White Bear or the Irish Pub where

Jürgen burst out one night with the news that Anke was expecting a baby. I congratulated them both and made a toast. Jürgen was already drunk. Anke was moved to tears.

7

During the afternoon, the people of Laun began to reclaim their town. As soon as the last of the German patrols had withdrawn back to the garrison, they gathered in the streets quietly, in small groups. Children came out to play on the square beneath the statue of the Czech martyr Johann Huss, which had ironically been allowed to stay untouched during the war.

Rumours went around about the uprising in Prague. About the imminent German capitulation. Men went up to the post office and began to throw stamps and registration forms into the street with a mixture of anger and joy. They had been given instructions by the National Committee at the U Somolu pub to repossess the institutions of the state. The officials who had been working at the post office up to then joined in, throwing documents out through the windows where they fluttered and chased each other in the street. Then the post office was closed for business.

The children who had come to watch this spectacle went back to the square to play, chasing, trying to take a scarf off each other. There were three girls and a boy; along with a dog who was trying to join in with their game. An over-friendly town dog who had always tilted his head and followed every inhabitant through the streets with equal curiosity, occasionally receiving a pat on the head from a German soldier, or the German woman in the red coat, coming from Mass. He was everybody's friend.

The idiocy of impartiality.

The dog chased the children around the square, keeping his eyes on the scarf, inevitably tearing at one of the girls' clothes instead of the scarf. The game was stopped and one of the older girls got cross, clouting him over the head. The girl whose dress was caught in the dog's mouth went on giggling as though she had been caught out as part of the game. When the dog eventually let go, the children tried to chase him away, but he stayed with them, at a distance, until they began to chase each other again and forgot that he was a dog. He was one of them.

Outside the pub U Somolu, where the National Committee was still in session, still negotiating with the Germans, a crowd, mainly men, had gathered to celebrate. They wanted to add voice to victory. They were told the pub was closed. It was too early to celebrate. Jaroslav Süssmerlich came out in person to explain that, if anything, things were going badly. The latest news from Prague was that German reinforcements were regaining control of the capital. The men outside announced their readiness to join the uprising by attacking the garrison. But the garrison held Czech hostages. An attack was impossible. Süssmerlich gave his men something else to do.

The people of the town went away and began to remove the German street signs, replacing them with rough, hastily painted Czech names on wood. They had reclaimed their town. Above the town, the sky was a celebration. From time to time, sunlight broke out over the hills, over the roof-tops of Laun, lighting up the calm columns of smoke like blue angels. There were no cars in Laun. Nobody owned very much. All they owned was their place in the world.

Some of the people went into the church to give thanks to God. Others went home to listen to the radio in groups, waiting for the Russian liberation. Others cooked food, fecklessly using up ingredients they might have rationed carefully for months up to then.

Before nightfall, a young couple arrived at the door of the pub asking to speak to the leader of the National Committee. They were told to go away. But they insisted.

'Just for one minute,' the girl said hopefully.

When they wouldn't go away, Süssmerlich finally agreed to speak to them. They had already received permission from their parents to marry. They had postponed the wedding for weeks, knowing it was wiser to wait for the end of the war. They had obtained permission from the priest in the town. All they needed now was permission from the National Committee. They wanted to marry the following morning.

Süssmerlich became angry.

'Can't you control your passions? The war is not over yet.'

But the intending couple returned some time later accompanied by the priest. The bride appealed with her eyes. The priest spoke on their behalf and explained that the couple wanted to get married on the day Czechoslovakia was liberated. On VE day.

Süssmerlich softened. Who could fail to understand such a request? He gave his permission and wished them luck in their lives. The couple thanked him. The priest blessed the revolution.

8

By evening, it was threatening to rain again. You could smell it in the air. And the clouds had built up over Bohemia.

Hauptmann Selders, having postponed his evening meal several times, finally took a late meal at his office. He would not go over to the officers' mess. The kitchen staff brought a table which they covered with a linen tablecloth. He ate his meal with some of the officers keeping him company.

In the next two rooms, the ongoing war was being monitored by Officer Kern and his radio operators. They listened to the German signal: Radio One from Prague. Someone else listened to the free Czech signal from Prague. Somebody kept tuning in to the BBC in London, who were giving almost live coverage of the Prague uprising. On another set, Officer Kern occasionally tuned in to Moscow. The news was getting worse.

After his dinner, Hauptmann Selders shared a glass of brandy with his officers. The kitchen staff came back and swiftly cleared away the table and the used plates.

Bertha, who had come back from her own evening meal, was also offered some brandy, but declined. It was a toast to the end. There was a peculiar atmosphere of calmness; camaraderie. Hauptmann Selders dropped his role as commander for a more friendly, fatherly tone and began to talk to everyone in the room about themselves.

There was a strange silence in the office. At any moment the phone could ring, or a technician could come in from the room next door with news that would change everything irreversibly. In spite of that, Hauptmann Selders asked each person what they would do after the war. He enjoyed listening to their plans, one by one. Officer Albert said he would go back and resurrect his father's printing business in Vienna. Officer Kern said he would join his wife in Nuremberg and start a gramophone shop. Others said they were keeping an open mind, perhaps business, perhaps a profession. One of them had already studied law. Bertha Sommer, surprised that she was asked at all, said she would hope to study medicine.

Hauptmann Selders revealed for the first time that he was an archaeologist before the war. He wished them well. Then he dismissed the gathering and told them all to get as much sleep as possible. A roster of officers would have to be selected to monitor events throughout the night. Bertha could stay in her room until morning, unless he sent for her.

Officer Kern volunteered to remain at his post, in the communications room. In the corridor, as the officers dispersed, Kern casually asked if his watch was showing the same time as everyone else's. Bertha looked at her watch. It was five to 10. And just when nobody was looking, Kern winked at her, pointing at his watch.

So the escape plan was on. Bertha crossed the square in a fever of excitement, not only at the thought of this clandestine and dangerous scheme, but at the idea of a man winking at her. It wasn't a suggestive wink, but a serious, conspiratorial sign. It had sent a rush of blood to her head. She was amazed how one signal like that from a man could make her feel so worked up and so secure at the same time. Whatever doubt she had about the plan was erased entirely with Kern's wink.

She looked around and saw the Red Cross vehicle by the gates. Once again, she remembered Kern's warnings. The fear of Russian captivity gripped her more than any other immediate fear.

She went to her room and sat down on the bed. She looked at herself in the mirror. She looked at her watch again and was afraid that an hour was too long to wait; she might change her mind again. By 11 o'clock, the inbred fear of the Reich might break out once more and restrain her. She thought of the most horrific sight she had seen, during the war, on her way to Prague; the sight from the train of men hanging, their heads bowed, arms limp, cardboard signs hung around them in warning to others.

She sat at the table and wrote in her diary to keep her mind off the worst. She put down a new heading: 'Evening 5 May'. She could put none of her real thoughts down. It would have left incriminating evidence. Not even Officer Kern's name. She looked around the room for something. She heard the rain beginning to fall outside the window and finally had something to write: 'Rain'.

It was the longest hour she had ever spent in her room. The months of waiting from January to May seemed to have been packed into that hour. She was clear in her mind what she was about to do. If they were caught, she would be punished as a deserter. Or aiding deserters. She could expect to be hanged. Under Schörner, there was no leniency. She was confused. Only the fear of the Russians convinced her to go ahead; to run.

When the time came, Bertha Sommer packed her diary in her bag and brushed her hair. She thought about perfume but decided against it. She put on her coat and hat, took a last look at the room and went out into the corridor, closing the door behind her. From one of the corridor windows she could see the Red Cross vehicle by the gates. The constant rain made it look further away. Kilometres away. A great rush of excitement hit the base of her stomach. She walked down the stairs and out through the door on to a porch where she was temporarily sheltered from the rain at least.

The rain bounced on the surface of the square. It beat down on every square inch of the roof and collected with a noisy gurgle in the drains.

There was nobody around as far as she could see. She decided that she would have to keep to the side of the buildings, both to avoid being seen and to avoid getting wet. She could go from one porch or doorway to the next. The rain made her think of her mother. What would her mother say? Bertha Sommer, what are you doing? You have never done anything illegal in your life. This felt suddenly like a great crime. She kept all doubts

32

away with the reminder of avenging Russians; merciless enemies. She put it out of her mind and tried to concentrate on getting across the square to the Red Cross vehicle.

She made it to the next doorway. She put her bag down on the ground and waited. She looked everywhere to see if anything moved. The rain was relentless. It would go on all night, it seemed, just like the night before.

Bertha blessed herself and ran to an arch next to the main administration building. From there she had a choice of going up a few steps and running along a raised wooden platform along the façade in front of the administration block, or along the square itself, in front of the platform. The raised porch or platform was sheltered by an awning, but its wooden boards might be far too noisy and arouse attention. She finally chose the square. But just as she had begun to run along the outside, she heard a door opening and saw extra light spilling out on to the square. If it wasn't for the railing, she would have been seen straight away.

She crouched down on the outside of the platform, getting soaked. She felt the rain getting in at the back of her neck. She saw the rain light up orange as it travelled past the light. She then heard Hauptmann Selders's voice. He was standing on the porch, condemning the weather. She couldn't move. She had no idea what to do. She knew her coat and her hat and her hair were getting soaked and realized how irrelevant it was. If she was caught there with her bag, she was finished.

Hauptmann Selders stayed on the porch gazing out at the rain. If he had looked down, he would have seen her. Every time she looked up, the strong rain blinded her.

Bertha crept slowly back towards the arch, holding her bag against her chest. She was ready to drop the bag. Ready to say she had come out because she felt ill. She made it back to the arch.

It was more than she could endure. With her back against the wall, she clutched the handles of her bag in her fist. Now, even the thought of Russian captivity seemed better than being caught there in the arch, with her bag, attempting to flee; a common deserter.

She had changed her mind. She was no good at breaking the law. You needed a devious mind. You needed to have done it before. She was weak. Certain that she had already been seen.

She heard the heavy sound of boots hurrying along the platform. A group of soldiers passed her by with their heads down against the rain. Just as they passed her hiding in the arch, they took a sharp turn and ran across the square away from her.

All Bertha Sommer wanted to do now was to get back to the safety of her room. The escape was far too risky, she decided. As soon as she heard the door to the administration block close, she checked the square and ran back to her own accommodation building.

Back in her room, she felt relieved. She took off her coat and her hat. Everything was soaked. She dried her hair. And slowly she began to regret that she hadn't gone the whole distance. She had gone so far. She was let down by her own fear and there was no way she would try it again. Her courage began to come back. But it was too late. She felt despair and anger at the fact that she had not made the escape with Kern. She felt she would never see home again.

Just before 11.45 she went out into the corridor to see if the Red Cross vehicle was still there. It was. She could see no movement around the vehicle. Once again she thought of making a run for it, abandoning all caution. But then she saw the vehicle lights come on. It began to move towards the gates. Then it was gone. Her chance had disappeared.

Bertha went back into her room and settled down for the night. She couldn't sleep. She could only think of Officer Kern waiting for her. She had let him down. He would surely think she had decided to remain loyal to the army. And he was the only man she could trust around here. Now she was on her own.

Finally, she fell asleep, only because she was exhausted and because the constant rain beating on the window mesmerized her.

In the morning, she got up and thought of the Red Cross car making its way towards the German border. She tried to visualize how far they would have got by now. She had a quick breakfast and reported for work early, at 5.45. The rain had eased off. It felt ridiculous to walk so confidently past the arch where she had been hiding only hours before.

Hauptmann Selders was already in his office surrounded by some of the officers. They were talking about Hriskov. The arms dump had fallen into Czech hands. During the night, soldiers had returned to the garrison on foot with the news. There was fighting to the north as well. She heard one officer come in with a report that one of the Red Cross vehicles had disappeared. Nothing more was said. She asked if there was anything she could do. She took the phone and tried to get a line to the capital.

An hour later, she got a real fright. Bertha couldn't tell whether she reacted with shock or sheer joy when she saw Officer Kern walk into the office with a report. German reinforcements had entered Prague and were set to regain control of the city. She ignored the information. She couldn't believe it was Officer Kern speaking. He had stayed behind. Why? She wanted to explain everything to him. But he went out again, avoiding her gaze.

It became clear that Kern had waited for her. Had he passed up a golden chance for her? To stay behind with her? The implication of such loyalty weighed on her thoughts.

9

The first time I went to Laun – now Louny – was late in 1985. First impressions are those of a sleepy town with a massive bus station which is completely out of proportion to the size of the town. The bleak tar-macadamed bus station offers little shelter except for a row of covered passenger islands. The bus routes which pass through the station give you some idea of the industry and crop farming in that part of Bohemia. It's like being dropped off at the edge of an industrial estate. I arrived there in the afternoon, in October, the best time to travel anywhere.

Around the bus station there was nothing but derelict land, overgrown with weeds. In the distance, I could see some isolated high-rise apartment blocks. The town itself had no colour. It's got an old square and a remarkable church. But it's not a place you would see on a tourist brochure. The people at the tourist office in Prague looked surprised that I wanted to go to Louny. What would a foreigner want in Louny? There were many places of interest, with ancient castles, like Kutná Hóra, or Karlovy Vary. And then there was Theresienstadt, not far from Louny, Czechoslovakia's Nazi transit camp where the ashes of 20,000 Jews were said to have been thrown in the river.

All I really wanted was to see Louny. There are places like that where you just want to be able to say: I've been there, I've seen the place.

There was little to see in Louny. Coming from West Germany, as I did, the place looked uninteresting, like a faded water-colour. The place that history left behind.

The shops were sparsely stocked with tins of beans and tins of stew. Everywhere in Czechoslovakia, I saw these neat pyramids of cans in the shop windows. There was a queue outside one of the shops in Louny. From Prague, I had learned that the sight of a queue was the sign of something worth buying. It seemed to be a bookshop.

I went into the pub U Somolu on the main street and had a drink, knowing that all Czech pubs have a habit of closing early. I would have spoken to some of the men in the pub, but they spoke neither English nor German and I didn't have a word of Czech. They looked at me. They must have wondered too what brought a German to Louny. I would like to have told them where I was really from. But it was too complicated.

I walked around the streets for a while. In the square, I sat down beside the statue of Johann Huss. The warm October sun hit the square at an angle. After a while the shadow of the buildings edged up across my face and reached the base of the façades on the other side. The loudspeakers which hung around the square suddenly came alive. First with a crackle and a lot of background noise, perhaps that of someone fumbling with the microphone, the voice eventually boomed out over the square. I had no idea what it was saying.

I tried some more people with English and received a bewildered stare each time. Then I wondered if this town, on the edge of the Sudetenland according to pre-war maps, might still have some old people who spoke German.

People shrugged a lot. I could see that they were dying to help me but were unable to. One man kept asking me questions enthusiastically in Czech. At the post office, somebody eventually pointed to an old woman who spoke a little German. I asked her about the garrison outside the town, at the top of the hill. She shook her head.

'You cannot go there,' she said. 'Nothing for tourists.' She waved her index finger.

I asked her what it was being used for. Who occupied it now?

'*Russen,*' she said.

It was not something she wanted to elaborate on. I had already asked too much. She walked away.

Since there was nothing else to do in Louny, I decided to walk back beyond the bus station up the hill to take a look at the garrison. It seemed like an impossible place to defend, surrounded only by a low wall and some rusted barbed wire. Around to the front of the garrison, along the wall, there was a large red star. That was as far as I went.

The journey back to Prague takes around an hour. The bus was full of workers commuting back to the towns along the way. A girl beside me kept falling asleep with her head repeatedly sinking on to my shoulder. Perhaps she was a factory girl. She wore overalls underneath her coat. Every now and again she woke up and realized that she had begun to lean against me. But she soon fell asleep again. Whenever the bus stopped, she sat up, startled, looking out through the windows as though she had gone too far.

10

According to the diaries of Bertha Sommer, an impeccably written account of the life of a young woman who reached the age of twenty when the Second World War started, she was born with a trinity of strong values: faith, honesty and cleanliness. There was nothing Bertha liked more than to wash her feet in the evening. She liked clean feet. Her faith and honesty helped her through what she called 'the turbulent times' in which she lived.

Born in the small Rhineland town of Kempen, she was brought up in a family devoted to the Catholic faith, except perhaps for her father, Erich, who was more devoted to cynicism and a good joke. In any case, both cynicism and Catholicism combined to place the family at odds with the new ideology of Nazism, and with the people in their town who had risen to prominence out of nowhere.

Up to then, Bertha's father had been a prominent businessman with a fine toy and stationery shop on the market square. He had a prodigious disregard for the most elementary notion of profit and loss. He refused to join what he called the 'Brown Wave'. His standing with the people of the town was based on the old values of gentlemanly wit. 'God save us from sudden wealth,' he would say, to the amusement of his followers, who shared his taste for wine, song and humour, along with his compulsion for practical jokes. One Sunday morning he borrowed a brown Nazi cap and climbed up to place it on top of the St George monument at the centre of the market square. Then he went and apologized for offending St George.

But Germany had lost its sense of humour. Nothing could save Erich Sommer from the plummeting Weimar economy, the accelerating age of fascism and his own progressive ill-health. The pulmonary illness which he had brought back from the First

World War got the better of him. He bowed out just before the Second World War, leaving behind his wife and five daughters, a trove of unsaleable toys, a hoard of initialled silver cutlery which was eventually sold off for nothing, and his inimitable sense of humour. Bertha writes how he asked her to bring him a mirror on his death-bed, where he looked at himself in silence for a long time before he said: '*Auf Wiedersehen, Erich.*'

With little else to share among them, the five sisters held on to some of their father's humour. They had a propensity to break down laughing, often until the tears rolled down their faces. His remarks were repeated as a comfort to their mother.

Bertha's mother, Maria, a professional opera singer who had given up her art for marriage, tried in vain to salvage the business. She resorted to giving singing and piano classes instead. If nothing else, the house was filled with laughter and music. Five girls and a mother who had once sung in the opera. They all sang arias, Schumann, hymns, love songs, pop songs like 'Lili Marlene', nursery rhymes – everything. In winter they placed a lighted candle into the grate to give students the illusion of warmth. But the demand for piano lessons had begun to diminish in a country preparing for war. The family eventually came to depend on social security under the new National Socialist state.

Life in Kempen became harder to explain. The Jews in the town disappeared. Families to whom Bertha had often been sent to buy gherkins had gone overnight. Once, on a trip to an aunt in Düsseldorf, Bertha records in her diary how she and her mother saw brand new shoes and leatherwear flung into the streets and how her mother said, 'What idiots. They'll regret this some day.' Shortly after that, the social security payments were mysteriously withdrawn from the Sommer family and life became impossible.

Plans had to be made to ease the burden. Grandmothers and aunts all conferred to make the best decisions for the five girls. Husbands were sought for the two eldest. The two youngest continued at school. Bertha, right in the middle, went to work as a secretarial assistant at the employment exchange, where she went on to obtain excellent references praising her enthusiasm and attractive manner. When the war came, her attributes were welcomed into the service of the army as part of the civilian personnel.

Bertha spent most of the time on the French coast of Normandy until the British arrived. She used the years in France to help her family, regularly sending home money to her mother and regularly arriving home with suitcases full of French fashions – dresses, blouses, hats, lingerie – all of which were quickly claimed by her sisters.

Shortly before D Day, she left France for the last time, with her cases stuffed to the gills. The trains were packed with girls coming home with their belongings, all evacuating back from the Normandy coast. The bombs were already raining on Germany. Bertha prayed hard. When they heard the planes overhead, she prayed for her life. And for her suitcases.

The first sight of bombed-out buildings and torn railway tracks came as a shock. It made the satin dress she was wearing at the time feel so inappropriate. She prayed it would be her last train journey of this war.

In the middle of the night, the train stopped very suddenly with a terrible jolt. Most of the girls were asleep, heads against shoulders, legs stretched out with travel-weary familiarity. Right in the middle of the country, the train stopped so suddenly that the girls were flung to the floor, into each other's arms or across each other. The lights went out. They could hear the sound of planes. Explosions of noise. Gunfire. In the distance, they saw the trail of anti-aircraft guns illuminating the sky. Nobody dared look out. Bertha found herself on the floor, underneath two others.

When the noise began to abate, an officer came through the carriage shouting at everyone to get out. The girls were all asking whether they should bring their cases. No luggage, the officer commanded.

They stepped down from the train and were all rushed into

the forest which ran along the tracks. They could smell the smoke. Further along the line, the sky was lit up by a burning train, a munitions train which had come under fire. The girls held to the edge of the forest for fear of partisans. The night was black. Three hundred women, two officers, a dozen recruits. The French train driver was bribed, or persuaded at gunpoint, to drive the empty train past the bombed-out munitions train. All the time, they heard the planes overhead. And they smelled smoke.

When they rejoined the train further along the track it was missing half its carriages. Bertha was fortunate to be reunited with her luggage. Many of the other girls never saw their things again. One of the officers assured them that the luggage would be sent on after them, but nobody believed him. As soon as they were gone, the carriages left behind would be looted and burned out by the French resistance. When the shortened train resumed the journey in the direction of Germany, it carried dozens of sobbing girls.

Bertha Sommer realized what it felt like to have luck on her side. She still had her three cases. And her life. All she had collected that night was a large pain in her right leg. Back in her seat she noticed the pain for the first time. Perhaps the sheer worry about survival was enough to anaesthetize it before that. When the train began to roll through the French night once more, Bertha finally got a chance to look at her leg. She rolled up her red dress and found a large blue bruise along the outside of her thigh. It was the size of a dinner plate, from the hip down, and around to her bottom. How it happened, she had no idea. She had no recollection of falling or banging into anything.

The girls in her compartment began to inspect her thigh. They had never seen such a big bruise before. How did it happen? It became a talking point. It was such a remarkable injury that the news travelled up along the carriages and Bertha repeatedly had to raise her dress to show other girls, bereaved girls whom she could not refuse. 'Mein Gott, Bertha!'

they all exclaimed, staring at her rich, dark bruise, the size of an oval-shaped platter under the yellowish light of the carriage.

More girls came to look. What beautiful underwear, too, one of them remarked. Bertha got fed up putting her leg on display. It was nothing, she said. A war souvenir. She only agreed to show it for the last time as a concession to the Frühling sisters, who had lost everything somewhere on the edge of the forest near Liège. And while Bertha raised her dress once more, an officer passed by and put his head into the compartment.

'Looks very nasty,' he said, smiling.

Bertha was startled to hear his voice. She pulled her dress down and sat in her seat, refusing to look at the officer. He moved on after one of the girls said it was all right. Bertha was shocked to think that she had shown her bruise to a man. An officer. On a train.

11

Anke's baby boy arrived in October, just after I had left on that trip to Czechoslovakia. I was away for a month in all, because I stopped in Nuremberg as well on the way back. As soon as I got back to Düsseldorf I found the card from Anke and Jürgen Lamprecht in the post. It was a printed card with a drawing of a stork carrying a baby bearing the announcement of their son Alexander.

I rang Anke at home to congratulate her. Anke rang me back later that same morning and arranged to meet me at a café in the centre of town.

She embraced me as usual, officially. She smiled that half-smile, but I could see she had something serious on her mind. Maybe I thought she looked a bit pale. We sat down for coffee outside a restaurant on the main shopping street. The weather was still quite warm. Why hadn't she brought the baby for me to see? She said I would have to drop around myself, some evening. She would arrange it. After that, Anke was unusually quiet.

I began to talk about my trip to Prague. I told her how I had found a restaurant there with a bar of soap chained to the sink in the wash-room. And how the restaurant served a variety of dishes, including liver soup and a dish called 'Ovary'. I took out a present of a Czech tube of toothpaste which I said I had bought especially for her. It was as hard as a metal bar. Normally Anke would have laughed at that. She said nothing. She looked at the toothpaste and then placed it on the table beside her coffee.

'What's wrong?' I asked.

Anke started crying. She cried to herself almost. As though she was alone.

What struck me as remarkable was that Anke never moved. She didn't move her hands to stop the tears. She stayed sitting back, legs crossed, arms languishing over the armrests, allowing the tears to run down her face as though it was perfectly normal. It was as though there was nobody around. Then she began to explain quite rationally that there was something wrong with the baby.

'Alexander has Down's Syndrome,' she said, making the first effort to remove the tears with a finger. Finally, she took a Kleenex from her bag.

I said I was sorry. I took her hand and said it again. I could think of nothing else to say. At the table next to us, there were two old women who kept looking at Anke. One of them had one of those little Spitz dogs tied on a lead to the leg of the table. He too was looking up at us, and when I looked back at him, he barked. I felt like kicking him.

I asked questions. Said some more ineffectual things and told Anke not to blame herself. She seemed not to hear me. She asked if these things usually skip a generation or what? I had no answer. I eventually took her back to her car and watched her drive away, crying.

Jürgen rang me a day later with a complete medical analysis. He could cope with it better. He was used to it as a doctor, as a gynaecologist. He told me straight out, there was no logic to it. But they would care for Alexander like any other child. No question. They would love him all the more.

Then he announced that Anke and himself had decided to move to Münster, where he was going to take over his father's practice. It seemed like the right decision.

A month later, they were gone.

12

The trains still ran in the Reich. Through the latter part of the war, Bertha Sommer got to see every part of Germany from the windows of a train, travelling from one post to the next, hoping, like most other German girls, to avoid being sent to the Eastern Front. At one point, Bertha managed to feign an illness which kept her at home for some months. Late in 1944, when she could no longer get away with it, she was sent to a large camp outside Hamburg where thousands of young German women waited to be posted, mostly to Poland and Russia. Rumours went around that women had to dig the trenches. In Russia, the German girls were already knee-deep in mud.

Bertha was lucky, so far. It was God on her side. She delayed wherever she could. In December 1944 she stretched her Christmas leave and arrived two days late in Salzburg to find that her group had already departed for the East. Her name was on the missing list. She met with the anger of officers who didn't know what to do with her and was eventually sent to Prague on New Year's Eve.

There was frost everywhere. The journey continued in the afternoon, when Bertha was put on a train and placed in a compartment with a young soldier. The compartment was locked. There was no heating on. She had disobeyed the orders of the Reich and could only expect the worst.

It was only when the train had been rolling for a while through the white land that she looked around her and discovered that the soldier with her in the compartment was no more than fifteen or sixteen. He was chained to the seat. A deserter. It made her feel like a deserter too. During the entire journey, neither of them spoke a word, each fearing that the other was an informer, or that a normal conversation would

46

combine them in some conspiracy. Bertha was afraid.

'What did we imagine?' she later wrote in her diary. 'Our fears were simple and absolute . . .

'Every time I wanted to go to the bathroom I had to call the guard to unlock the door. It made me feel like a criminal. Every time the boy had to go, they unlocked his chains and went with him. Were they afraid he would throw himself off the train? He was so young. He had just begun to grow a moustache. The whole idea was so idiotic. The effort to get this boy back to the Front took up the full attention of three grown-up soldiers.'

Somewhere along the way, at a small station in the mountains, the train stopped for a long time, at least an hour. There were trees all round, heavy bags of snow weighing on the branches. When the train moved on slowly, they moved past a timber-yard at the back of the station where Bertha saw something she never forgot.

She looked away at first and couldn't believe it. Then she looked again before the train moved along behind a large timber-shed and straight into the woods again. There in the yard she had seen three men hanging from an improvised scaffold. She saw them long enough to believe it. Their bodies were limp. Their heads hung down as though they were asleep or something. They wore civilian clothes and had cardboard signs around their necks. Some soldiers stood around the yard, looking on. Smoking. Or maybe it was their breath. There was no breath from the men hanging.

It was the only time that Bertha's eyes fully met those of the recruit in the carriage with her. He had obviously seen it too, and a stark acknowledgement flashed between them until they remembered their own situation and ignored the brief contact again.

Bertha could not help thinking about it as the train rocked along through the white landscape, through a German fairytale. Had they done that for Germany? For her? All the time, as the train sped on towards Prague, she kept repeating her own secret name for that day in her mind. The Timber-yard of silent breath.

47

With a combination of fury and fear, she repeated the title in her head like a lullaby, trying to keep a nightmare away. Later, she changed it again. It became: the Timber-yard of breath.

The journey took sixteen hours. For a long time, she was unable to eat the sandwiches she had brought with her. She felt sick. She was also afraid to share her food with the nameless soldier in her compartment. Only when it was dark did she decide to eat furtively, avoiding any eye contact. She ate alone, chewing quietly. The food soon gave her a warm feeling. But it felt all wrong. In the dark, she leaned over and placed a sandwich made of black bread and cheese on the seat beside the soldier. The boy took the sandwich without a word. Their silent chewing was like a coded conversation.

The train arrived in Prague early in the morning on New Year's Day. The boy was led away, handcuffed to another soldier.

At the time, Bertha's own luck seemed more important to her. But in the subsequent months while she was stationed in Laun, it played on her mind. The men hanging. And the young soldier chained to the seat. She should have spoken to him. Asked his name. Encouraged him. Memorized his address so that she could send word to his mother for him. But there were always other things which took over. Other personal fears.

'We were all fed on fear,' she wrote in her diary.

13

I kept in touch with Anke and Jürgen. On the rare occasions that they came back to Düsseldorf on a weekend, they came to visit me. Once every two years only. We would spend the night out in a restaurant talking, drinking. We kept in touch by post mainly. Or by phone. Every year I sent a gift for Alexander on his birthday: 1 October. And Anke would write me a short, impulsive letter back just to let me know they were alive. If I didn't get a letter I could expect a call sooner or later.

They were very happy in Münster. Jürgen was doing extremely well in his father's practice. Though Anke sometimes complained that she didn't see enough of him. And occasionally, she hinted that she would like to be back in her city for a while. But Jürgen would never move back to Düsseldorf. Anyway, it was out of the question because of the new practice.

Once, Anke sent a photograph of herself and Alexander to keep me up to date. She hadn't changed a bit. Though I would not have said that in a letter. My letters were strictly neutral. They were addressed to both Jürgen and Anke, usually in that order. The kind of neutral letters which are read out over the breakfast table before they collect jam stains. This is one of her letters. It was sent when Alexander was three years old. Far from neutral, I thought.

Got your present for Alex, thank you very much. Though I don't quite know what he is going to do with it. All toys eventually drive us mad because it only reminds us of his limitations. A toy is like a test to a child's limits. The joy that most parents get is watching their children break down those limits. Jürgen and I, we have to make exceptions for everything. Of course I'm very grateful that you remember Alexander's birthday like this every year. Sometimes I get the urge to talk to somebody else about our life, somebody outside the family, somebody not directly involved . . .

Anke had never said anything like this to me about Alexander's difficulties before. She would never even refer to his having Down's Syndrome. She had told me that Alexander was going to a special school, and occasionally described his retardation and lack of progress on the phone when I asked her, but she always painted a picture of extreme patience. I would never have thought she was anything less than completely happy. It came as a total surprise. The letter ended like this:

Sometimes I want to be back in Düsseldorf. Or in the Eifel. I think about you. I think about my other life.

Anke

14

On 6 May, the German Army was still in occupation at Laun. And they still occupied the protectorate of Czechoslovakia. By a thread.

Overnight, German planes had flown over the capital of Prague raining down leaflets appealing to the inhabitants to submit, or pay for it in blood. The leaflets promised that no Czech would be harmed and that the German Army wished only to engage the real enemy: the Red Army. Later on, the same planes flew over Prague again with a more persuasive message: phosphor bombs. SS units with tanks approached from the south to regain control of the city, following orders literally: 'the whole nest has to burn'.

In Laun, the German Wehrmacht training garrison became actively involved in the war for the first time. Early that morning, local observers from the town posted to watch the garrison overnight came back to report to the committee at the U Somolu pub that large troop movements were seen leaving in the direction of Hriskov. At least six or seven trucks full of soldiers. There was nothing the committee could do but warn the people at Hriskov by phone. Nothing Laun could do but wait.

Bertha Sommer had not been up to see Hauptmann Selders give the order to send out troops. She arrived to find the office in a frenzy of activity. She was there in time to see the trucks leaving; in time to feel a futile compassion for all those young recruits heading in the direction of the fighting. South. East. Into the hands of the Red Army.

Bertha had given up her own final chance to escape the end. But instead of becoming dismal, she decided to become useful. She took up the task of keeping in touch with other garrisons around Bohemia, to see what their information was. Garrisons like Trutnov, which had also taken a stand against the Czechs with hostages.

It became clear by now that Officer Franz Kern had begun to play the most important role of all. As radio engineer, he was the lifeline to the outer world. Every twenty minutes, he appeared in the office with fresh news. Reports from Prague or from Moscow; sometimes even as far away as London.

Bertha had not spoken to him since their escape failed. She wanted to catch his eye, to get some acknowledgement. She wanted to let him know that she had tried to escape with him the night before. It was the rain. She wanted him to know that she had not informed on him. But Officer Kern seemed too preoccupied. Their eyes met only in passing. There was no communication between them. No signal.

When she eventually found an excuse to go out into the corridor, she was hoping to catch him and speak to him briefly. With the Third Reich collapsing around them, she invented a reason to meet him alone for a moment, but he would not let her speak. He placed his index finger over his lips. He didn't want to hear.

'I know,' was all he said.

That was enough for Bertha. What it was he knew wasn't clear. But he must have known that she had not betrayed him. She went back to her work.

During the day, the activity in the office intensified apace with the war outside. There was talk of capitulation. But General Schörner wanted more valour and sent out personal messages to his men over the radio: '*Soldiers. You must break every resistance from the Czechs with the heaviest weapons.*'

Very soon after that, Officer Kern came back into the office with another message, this time broadcast by the free Czech radio. It had been put out repeatedly in three different languages: '*Prague calling. Here is free Prague. Red Army – send help. We need tanks and planes. Don't let us go down in a useless struggle. Help, quick, quick, quick.*'

It is significant that Prague began to call on the Russians, instead of the Americans, who had been closer to Prague for days. At one point, a report broadcast by the BBC in London said that the American Army at Pilsen had begun to move on Prague. But the report was misleading. Nothing could lure the Americans to get involved in what had already become a Soviet state.

For the Germans, it meant that all hope of surrendering to the Americans had faded. Second best, they would have to surrender to the Russians.

15

That evening, straight after dinner, Bertha Sommer went to her room to rest. There was nothing she could do at the office any more. She took her washbag and towel and went to the wash-rooms on her landing to wash her hair, and after that her feet. She had just got back to her room when she heard footsteps in the corridor outside her door. She could hear a knock on the room next door which she knew to be unoccupied. She stopped combing her hair and listened. When there was no answer, the footsteps came and approached her own door. She waited for the knock and then went to answer it, opening up a little so that only her face could be seen around the door. It was Officer Kern.

'Ah, Fräulein Sommer. I didn't know which room was yours. I've got to speak to you for a moment.'

She didn't know whether this was an order or a request. This was not a good idea, his coming to her room, she thought. She looked past him to see if there was anyone else in the corridor. But the building had been largely empty since the civilian popu-lation moved out. Her hair was wet and she stood there feeling awkward in her dressing-gown and slippers, waiting for him to speak. She was glad at last to be able to explain to him what happened the night before, but felt it wouldn't be right to invite him inside.

'I'm afraid we might be overheard in the corridor,' he said. 'I won't stay long, Fräulein Sommer, I promise.' He understood her reluctance.

'Wait. Let me get dressed.'

He stood outside and heard her moving around inside the room. As soon as he heard the sound of clothes, he began to pace up and down to give her complete privacy. Bertha checked herself in the mirror and considered the implications of letting a man into her room. The war is a time for exceptions. She looked around to make sure that the room was tidy and reminded herself not to speak too soon. Let him speak first, she said to herself.

'Forgive me, Fräulein Sommer,' Kern said as he entered the room. 'But I felt I had to speak to you. What happened last night doesn't matter.'

'I tried to go,' she broke in, already disregarding her own first rule.

'I know,' he replied. 'I saw you. I saw you turn back. You were right. There was no other way. I was worried that somebody else might have seen you too. Now I'm sure nobody did.'

'I saw the Red Cross vehicle leave.'

'Yes,' Officer Kern said. 'It doesn't matter. What happens now is more important. It is too dangerous to make any new plans to escape. We should wait for a ceasefire and hope for the best. I know the Red Army is approaching from the north. They're not far away. But our best bet is to stay. The hostages here give us some protection.'

Bertha was taken aback by the way Officer Kern included her so presumptuously in his plans. At the same time it reassured her. There was something she wanted to ask him, but she had forgotten what. She let him speak.

'There is great hostility against the Germans. I've heard reports from London about . . . terrible things. About the Jews in the camps. I thought it was all propaganda at first. But now, I'm beginning to believe it. No imagination could invent what they're saying about us.'

Officer Kern checked himself. It was not something he wanted to talk about. He had listened to the radio too much.

'I'm sorry. Fräulein Sommer, the last thing I want is to alarm you, but when this war is over, even when the ceasefire is called, I know the Russians won't stop. They will overrun all of Czechoslovakia and take as many of the German troops as possible. Hauptmann Selders is playing a clever game with the hostages. Maybe that will save us. But after that, it's every man for himself.'

Officer Kern spoke as though he had seen everything happen before.

'Fräulein Sommer, I want you to know that the bicycle is at your disposal.'

Bertha laughed. Maybe it was a nervous laugh. She felt she had done him an injustice, and tried to be serious. But the idea of fleeing from the Russians on a bicycle seemed too funny. Officer Kern smiled.

'I'm sorry,' Bertha said. 'I'm only laughing at the idea of trying to escape on a bicycle.'

'Believe me, Fräulein Sommer, when this war is over, the roads from here to Kempen will be so stuffed with people, nothing will move faster than a tortoise. In fact, it is my guess that the bicycle will be the fastest mode of transport. Believe me, when they call a ceasefire, every cart with wheels left on it will be out there going home.'

Bertha felt the intimacy by which he spoke the name of her home town, Kempen. She thanked him. It was as though he had undertaken to deliver her home to her family. Officer Kern said he would make all the arrangements to get the bicycles put on trucks for the first part of the journey to Eger. The Americans were at Eger, he said. She thanked him again, placing all her faith in him. She wanted to tell him that with her prayers and his intuition, they would both get home safely. But then she remembered once more that he was standing in her room.

It was awkward. A man in her bedroom. Then she remembered what it was she wanted to ask.

'Why did you stay?'

He looked puzzled. Perhaps he hadn't thought of an answer yet.

'Why didn't you leave when you had the chance?'

'I couldn't,' he said. 'To be honest, I had second thoughts.'

Officer Kern hesitated. The subject made him uneasy. He chose his words carefully.

'When you didn't arrive, when I could see that you weren't coming, I thought about it again. I felt I would not only be letting you down, but everyone else in the garrison as well. I thought about it all last night. I felt I would have betrayed everyone, not the Fatherland or Germany or anything like that; not the Reich, that doesn't matter to me or to anyone now. No, I thought it would have been cowardly to leave. I felt it was not the right time to betray, just hours before the end.'

He stopped. He could have gone on spilling forth his reasons. He looked at her and decided to be lighthearted instead.

'. . . And as well as that, the weather wasn't very good.'

Bertha laughed.

'Now, if you forgive me, I must go back to work,' Kern said, looking around the room. He saw her bag on the table and said, 'I see you're packed. Very good.'

Bertha nodded. It was a private matter whether or not she was packed, but she said nothing.

Officer Kern moved towards the door, but instead of opening it himself, he allowed her to open it and peer into the corridor to see if anyone was out there. All clear. She let him out and felt there was something terribly clandestine about doing so. Something which bound them together in a subversive liaison.

'Sleep well,' he whispered.

'Good night,' she replied, as officially as possible. Sleep was not the right word.

16

By the time Bertha woke up the following morning of 7 May, the German High Command had surrendered officially on all fronts. The ceasefire was set for midnight of the next day, the 8th. They could fight away to their hearts' content until then. General Schörner again didn't agree, and sent out a radio broadcast saying that reports of capitulation were nonsense. During the morning the Americans personally flew a German messenger from the German High Command into Prague airport in order to convince Schörner to give it up. He didn't. SS men went on the rampage in the city, killing and ordering civilians to dismantle the 2,000 barricades they had put up in the streets.

The battle for the Hriskov arms dump was eventually won by the German troops from Laun around midday on the 7th. But it was an empty victory because they immediately began to flee back to Laun from the approaching Russians, leaving dozens of dead and wounded comrades as well as Czech insurgents behind them.

Sometime during the day, General Schörner took a plane and flew to Austria, where he crash-landed and handed himself over to the Americans, leaving his troops still fighting off the Red Army.

Nobody slept much the next night either. After the ceasefire at midnight, the Czechs were told to shoot only when fired on.

On the following morning, the 8th, the Germans in Prague eventually agreed their own ceasefire with the Czechs. The terms were such that the troops would keep their weapons until they got to the German border. They would not sabotage the weapons but would leave them by the roadside along with all ammunition. The retreating German troops would take only enough food to last the journey and leave everything else intact behind them. In return, the Czechs would allow them to retreat unhindered. The people in the towns would make way for a peaceful withdrawal.

By early morning, the first trucks began to move out of the garrison at Laun. The square was filled with the smell of diesel. The first and last trucks of the convoy carried Czech hostages. Bertha Sommer and Officer Franz Kern were somewhere in the middle. Kern was still monitoring the radio to keep the units informed about the position of the Russians. They were coming from the north and could only be around thirty kilometres, even less, behind them.

The convoy of trucks drove through the town of Laun and out along the road to Postelberg. The people of Laun came out to see them leaving. Some of the men had thrown out the old German street signs, forcing the German trucks to pass over them. A small group of women and children stood on the square, watching. They had really gathered there to welcome the liberating Red Army, who were expected to arrive very soon. The people were silent, waiting to cheer the arrival of the Russians. The only one smiling was a boy with Down's Syndrome standing with his mother in the square, waving his hand with excitement at the German trucks as they disappeared out of the town.

The roads were already crowded with people on the move. Everything moved slowly.

Around lunchtime, the hostages were released in the town of Postelberg, about twenty kilometres away. Officer Kern heard further reports on his field radio that the fighting in Prague was continuing. The Germans were bombing the city from the air. One radio report said the Hradčany palace in Prague had been deliberately set on fire by the SS. But this turned out to be false.

Officer Kern then heard a message go out to the Czech people telling them to clear the way for the Russian troops so that they could head off the German withdrawal. The free Czech radio appealed to the Russians to give chase.

'Catch the German murderers and kill them if they resist.'

17

I didn't get back to Czechoslovakia again until October 1989. Nothing had changed. If anything, the place had become more and more bleak and despondent. There was no energy. The wildest imagination could not predict the fall of communism.

But there were signs of change in Prague. The city was already full of East Germans escaping on the freedom trains to the West. The West German embassy was besieged by young people climbing over the fences. No régime could fight off the lure of the free market. TV enlightenment. It was like forcing people to believe the earth was flat when every small child knew it was round. In Czechoslovakia, they still had to believe the lie. Perhaps the memory of tanks on Wenceslas Square in 1969 was still too vivid. Prague was still paralysed by silence, by fear and by the dim yellow lighting in the streets. Nobody could imagine change. Nobody, except maybe the young students with their candles and guitars quietly congregating on the Karls Bridge; too young to remember tanks.

I looked over the bridge into the Vltava. As with most rivers, I wondered how many people had fallen in or been thrown in over the years. At night, it looked black, under the illuminated façade of the Hradčany palace.

I had spent the afternoon in the most under-used building in Prague – the Museum Klementa Gottwalda, named after the founder of the modern communist state of Czechoslovakia. It seemed like the last place anyone would want to visit. The posters and postcards on sale at the reception inside all bore stern faces of idealists, men and women at work on tractors or in factories under blazing red banners. An impervious old woman sitting in her apron behind the reception desk interrupted her knitting to listen to my requests. I was looking for information on the Second World War resistance movement in Louny. Safe information about an old revolution that was fifty years in the past by now. They found an old man with a pipe who was only too happy to dig out the files for me.

The bars in Prague closed around 9. I spent the evening walking through the poorly lit squares and medieval streets looking for one that was still open. Like most tourists, I crossed the Karls Bridge five or six times, back and forth. All the time I heard the footsteps of pedestrians. It's the one thing you remember about Prague; the sound of feet.

At a bar below the Hradčany palace I met a man called Mírek who told me there was no point even talking about freedom in Czechoslovakia. Why depress yourself with the thought? He changed the subject to talk about writers. He had read all the banned Czech writers in dog-eared photocopied editions passed around furtively at the university. He dismissed them, throwing his arms out towards a group of vociferous drinkers at the next table. They all talk like that around here, he said. We're all quasi-philosophers.

I took the bus to Louny the following day. Nothing had changed there either in the last four years, except for one thing. The town had a new building. Right across the road from the bus station, and equally out of proportion with the rest of the town, they had erected a large red-brick office block. It turned out to be the headquarters of the Communist Party in the Louny district, and had the familiar red star over the entrance.

The town itself was as grey and dismal as before. This time, it seemed colder. Once again, I made attempts to speak to people in German, in English, in sign language. At the post office several people shrugged their shoulders. In the square, a young woman with a pram almost ran away to avoid me. An old man eventually directed me straight back to the Communist Party headquarters, the spanking new building at the end of the main street.

Inside, at a desk behind a glass cage, sat a porter. Why they put him behind glass was difficult to understand. He came out to speak to me and understood enough German to make out that I was not just lost or nosy. The idea of a tourist in Louny defies logic. I made it clear that I had a purpose. He called various people out of their offices to come and look at me. Perhaps it was a stroke of luck that the head of the Communist Party at Louny happened to walk in right then, a man with bushy eyebrows, in the mould of Brezhnev, with a soft spot for the subject of resistance. Within minutes, the whole party apparatus swung into action.

I was taken upstairs and given tea. A network of historians were contacted by phone. They sent for the best expert on the resistance movement in the region of Louny: Mrs Marie Sekalova. But as she didn't speak German or English, they had to send for the town archivist, Dr Milan Houdek, who could speak thirteen languages.

An hour later, I was walking back up to the town square in the company of Mrs Sekalova and Dr Houdek, followed into the archives building by the eyes of local people. Mrs Sekalova was a small, intense woman. She had brought some books and magazines with her. We sat around a map of the region, which I had spread out on a coffee table in Dr Houdek's office. Mrs Sekalova began to re-enact the liberation of Czechoslovakia from the fascists. Milan Houdek translated.

I made a small X mark on the map near Hriskov. Another X at Postelberg, now called Postoloptry, where the Czech hostages were released. Mrs Sekalova showed pride and pleasure at the task of digging out these forgotten facts. Then I discovered why she was so pleased. She had met Jaroslav Süssmerlich in person: the leader of the National Committee at Louny. And her own father had been among the resistance fighters around Hriskov. She had spoken to many of the people involved and had personally recorded eye-witness accounts. I asked her if she would mind telling me how old she was in 1945, when all this happened. She was four. She remembered standing on the square with her mother, watching the German troops pulling out. The facts were close to her heart.

18

The facts were as follows:

6 May: Early morning, six trucks left the German garrison for Hriskov, where fighting took place from early afternoon until noon of the 7th, when the Germans repossessed the arms dump. The number of dead found on the 8th were thirteen Czechs and sixteen Germans. The injured casualties on both sides were taken to the Louny *Gymnasium*, where they lay side by side, treated by Czech doctors. The arms dump itself was found abandoned.

8th May: The German Army left Louny at 7 a.m. in the direction of Postoloptry, where they released all hostages. Twelve hours later, the first Russian troops rolled into Louny, at 7.15 p.m. At 8 p.m. the same day, German soldiers (presumed to be those returning from Hriskov) were engaged by the Russians at Clumchany on the outskirts of Louny, where the last exchange of fire was recorded in the region.

In Prague, the shooting continued into 9 May, with bands of SS men disregarding the ceasefire from midnight of the 8th. German planes continued to bomb a number of towns in north Bohemia on the 10th.

The last bastion of the Reich in the west was the North Sea island fortress of Heligoland, which surrendered to the British Navy on the 11th. The last battle on Czech soil was fought near Příbram, where the SS units fleeing from Prague were hoping to surrender to the Americans but ran into the Russians instead. The final exchanges in Czechoslovakia were recorded at Příbram on 11 May. A monument stands there to mark the end of fighting. The last German Wehrmacht units under arms are believed to have surrendered at the Yugoslav town of Slovenski Gradek on 15 May.

I was still looking for the last shot.

Mrs Sekalova had trawled through her material and we called it a day. Outside in the square, the loudspeakers had begun to resound like a curfew. Dr Houdek promised to send on any further information by post. We began to move towards the door.

The only thing I still had to see before I left Louny was the church. The St Nicholas church. It was famous for something or other, I asked? Dr Houdek confirmed that it was famous for its wooden altar carving.

The three of us walked across the square in the direction of the church. The loudspeakers fell silent. The square was empty except for the statue of Johann Huss. Dr Houdek began to speak more openly when he got outside. He seemed to have no fear while he spoke in English. Nobody in Louny could guess what he was saying and it became like a secret language almost. He had learned English from books and tapes; from the Beatles, and John Lennon. He spoke out as though he wanted to show me how free he really was.

Mrs Sekalova walked silently beside us. She smiled every time our eyes met. She was greeted courteously by other people passing by. It became clear how important she was in the town; a woman of great standing.

We climbed the steps of the church. Dr Houdek went ahead and opened the big oak door. I held the door open for Mrs Sekalova who had not come all the way up the steps yet. I noticed a reluctance, as though she wanted to go home. Perhaps she had work to do; children, dinner, to think of.

Seeing that I was still holding the door for her, she came up and entered the church. Dr Houdek had already gone to talk to the priest, who came back with him, switching on every light in the church in order to illuminate the great carving. It was a source of local pride, Dr Houdek explained, even though the carving was somewhat out of place and more appropriate in a larger architectural setting. Once more, Dr Houdek displayed the freedom of his critical faculties in a language that nobody in Louny could grasp.

Mrs Sekalova had withdrawn into the background. She had hardly even come into the church properly and I took it she was becoming more and more anxious to get back to her own duties. She lingered at the door.

The priest came over and whispered to Dr Houdek before he went around switching the lights off again.

'The priest does not like Mrs Sekalova to be here,' Dr Houdek said to me quite openly. 'Mrs Sekalova is a big communist. The church does not like the communists.'

I turned around and saw that Mrs Sekalova was gone.

'They have asked me to be a communist too,' he went on, nodding towards the door. 'I refused. I don't like the communists either. They keep asking me to join the party, otherwise I will not be able to keep my job in the archives. I think they are going to make things difficult for me.'

The priest had plunged the church into gloom. Only the light left on the altar fell on the rows of benches.

'I have a good job here. But now I think I will lose my job because I will not be a communist.'

Outside, Mrs Sekalova stood at the bottom of the steps, waiting. I was glad she hadn't rushed off. We shook hands. She said something in Czech that I could not understand. All I could do was to answer in English. But then Dr Houdek translated. Mrs Sekalova wished to invite me back to Louny for the big celebrations in May the following year.

Dr Houdek walked with me back to the bus station. We passed his house on the main street of Louny, Leninova 95. It used to be called Prag Strasse. He said he would write to confirm the facts.

It was late when I got back to Prague that night. Too late to have a drink. The hotels were full of East Germans fleeing to the West. When I arrived back at my own hotel, the Intercontinental, I noticed that the large vertical neon sign was missing the R and the C. The Soviet Union was cracking up.

I sent some postcards while I was there. As usual, I wrote the same thing on each, hoping the recipients wouldn't run into one another. I had bought six postcards showing the magnificent interior of the Klementa Gottwalda museum, draped with red flags and dripping in chandeliers.

I thought of the novel by Kundera where somebody is hounded for sending an anti-state joke on a postcard. I was curious to see if the joke still worked in the autumn of 1989, and sent six Klementa Gottwalda interiors with the same remark on the back: 'Never trust a comrade.'

I wasn't thinking. One of them went out to Jürgen and Anke in Münster.

19

Before I left Czechoslovakia, I wanted to buy a gift for Alexander. Anke had written to me telling me that Alex was very ill. Something serious. I had deliberately not sent him a gift on his fourth birthday because I had already promised Anke I would visit them when I got back from Czechoslovakia. I wanted to bring him back something from Prague.

A spinning top was all I could find. At a small kiosk in the main train station, I found this Czech-made spinning top. The rather corpulent man in the kiosk reluctantly took the toy out of the box to let me see it. It looked like a decent spinning top, but I still wanted to be sure I wasn't buying junk and demanded to see what the colours were like. I asked the man to spin it for me, making a whirlpool sign with my finger. The colours were impressive, merging from pink to azure, purple to scarlet. It didn't hum. But there was something comical about a large, angry man inside a tiny kiosk at this vast Soviet railway station, pumping a spinning top. He did it with deep resentment. He hated the customer.

I bought it. On the train afterwards I reconsidered, wondering if the spinning top was the right thing for Alex, for a four-year-old boy with Down's Syndrome. Would Anke and Jürgen be happy with it?

You think too much on trains.

I spent thirteen hours on the train before I reached Nuremberg, late in the evening. Re-entering Germany was like falling over a cliff into another world; a world where everybody loves the customer. The main streets were bursting with neon lights and brightly lit window displays. There was already a hint of Christmas.

I rang Anke the next day and told her I would go straight up to Münster to see them. I continued the journey across Germany late at night on the Intercity. I saw people taking out flasks of coffee and sandwiches; eating quietly by themselves. I saw people asleep with their mouths open. Sometimes I could make out a succession of electricity pylons in the dark landscape. In Frankfurt main station, where I waited to change trains, I saw a group of American GIs, two blacks and three whites, all drunk and cheerful. They were just beginning to grow moustaches. I saw one of them stuff a half-eaten hamburger down another GI's neck. 'You motherfucker,' I heard the guy say, while the others fell about laughing. I felt at home.

By the time it got bright, I was passing along the Rhine. It was a still, wintry Sunday morning. An elderly woman got on and sat by the window in my compartment. Nobody talked. Everybody stared out of the window at the rust-coloured landscape.

A while later, an argument developed between the old woman and the Intercity conductor. He accused her of not paying the Intercity surcharge. The woman pleaded with him, saying she had already paid it at her travel agent's. The conductor would not accept that and continued to demand 14 DM from her. She began to cry. I could see the tears on her face.

I intervened. I asked him if this was necessary. Did he not believe the woman? He refused to speak to me. He looked out of the window and demanded 14 DM. The Intercity conductor doesn't believe tears. He gave her a choice of paying up or handing over her identity card. She fumbled in her purse with the tears streaming down her face.

I talked to her afterwards. She stayed on the train until Duisburg, still in tears, still proclaiming the injustice. I began to think there was more behind this. Maybe she was really crying about something else. I wanted to ask her about the war. Where she had been. What her experiences were. I believe tears when I see them. All she would tell me was that she was on the way back from visiting relatives in Stuttgart. Some

68

people don't mind telling you things. Others will keep it to themselves. This frail woman sat in silence for the rest of the journey, staring out of the window.

20

I forget why Anke is beautiful. When you see her after a long time, you say to yourself, with a familiar shock: she is extremely beautiful. As much so in a pair of jeans and T-shirt as she would be dressed up to go out for an evening. Maybe it's a universal charm, crossing all boundaries of personal preference. Everybody likes her. She can get away with anything. She can do no wrong.

Is it some kind of perfect symmetry in her features? Is she like a model? No. In the mirror, she is a little off-centre. Her smile is left-seeking. That's the real test of symmetry, the one that artists use when painting portraits. Anke has idiosyncratic beauty. You would never guess her background. Or her age. She is one of those women who are beautiful as children and go on being so until they're eighty. She will be a lovely old woman. Her mother is the same.

Anke jumped out of the Mercedes and walked over to embrace me. She had that slanted smile on her face. Life is for a laugh was her leitmotif; always was. I threw my bag into the back beside the child seat. On the far side, there was a large box of disposable nappies. It made me calculate. Alexander was four. Still a baby.

It was like a homecoming. Anke drove slowly through the town, talking and asking questions. The old buildings of Münster were all lit up, light spilling over on to nearby trees. The streets were empty. Sunday evening. We stopped at traffic lights, where the red light bled on to a tree beside it. Anke kept talking and looking at me.

Jürgen had the door open when we arrived. He embraced me too and stepped back to take a good look at me, to see if I had changed.

'I got your card,' he said, punching me and then leading me away into the living-room with his arm around my shoulder.

Alexander was shy at first. Jürgen showed him how to shake hands. Then Alex wanted to shake hands again and again. He ran away and came back to say hello again. His eyes shone.

'I hope you've got some time,' Jürgen said. 'I hope you can stay for a while. We've got a lot to talk about. And I'm going to take you hang-gliding if you stay till next weekend.'

I told him I could stay only a few days. He said he was going to change my mind. Then he sat back and listened. Jürgen wanted to know everything.

Alex ran into the kitchen, where Anke was preparing something to eat. He came back moments later with an onion for me. After a while he came back again with an apple. His mouth dribbled.

Jürgen talked about his new practice. He had taken over his father's practice and moved into new premises. Then he began to talk about changes happening in Germany, about the freedom trains. Münster was full of East Germans and displaced Germans from Poland. What did freedom of choice mean in Germany? What did they want?

'It's the choice between thirty-five bars of soap,' Jürgen said. 'The choice between mauve and sludge-green blouses. The choice to boot down the *Autobahn* at a hundred and fifty kilometres an hour. Everybody wants that choice.'

Alexander had dragged a chair into the middle of the room and sat underneath it, pretending to go to sleep. He began to sing. It was more like groaning.

'Real freedom is a completely different matter,' Jürgen said. 'Something we can talk about later: the difference between state freedom and domestic freedom. Personal freedom.'

Over dinner, it was Anke's turn to talk about the events in Germany. People wanted the freedom to go anywhere in the world, even if they chose to stay at home.

On the wall of the kitchen hung a wooden plate with an egg-cup, spoon and a child's cup glued to it. Jürgen usually fed

Alex when he was home. He showed extreme patience. Alex was limited in what he could chew. He got distracted and he wanted to eat from Jürgen's plate or from my plate instead. Jürgen and Anke never talked about him in the third person when he was present. Jürgen held out the cup and Alex sang or sighed noisily as he drank. When he finished, there was a milk moustache on his upper lip.

After dinner I gave Alex the spinning top. It drove him mad. At first he got very excited about it when Jürgen spun it for him. But then he tried it himself and the handle broke off. He began to wail. Jürgen took him on his knee while I fixed the spinning top. But Alex was tired. He kept crying. I could see the full extent of his deformities; the pronounced cast in his eyes, the ill-fitting teeth and his inability to understand.

21

Bertha Sommer never saw the hostages being released. She never caught sight of their faces or of anyone getting off the trucks in Postelberg. All she saw were the onlookers in the streets and the occasional glimpse of purple lilac in full bloom as the trucks moved on again. The summer had come. It was hot on the trucks, under the green tarpaulins, as they drove out of Czechoslovakia. At times the trucks were hit by a shower of rain, but the sun quickly came out again. There was a smell in the trucks, like the inside of a marquee tent. There was also a constant smell of diesel.

After Postelberg, things moved slower than ever. Sometimes the pace was reduced to no more than five or ten kilometres an hour. Every conceivable form of transport was out on the roads, every available set of wheels; carts, barrows, prams, on the move. Outside Postelberg, they were held up for almost an hour.

The German units from Laun were determined to stay together as one convoy. Everywhere, Sudetenland civilians attached themselves to the retreat, getting in between the trucks, sometimes separating part of the convoy. Whole families were fleeing to Germany. Families pleading to be taken on the trucks. They knew what was going to happen. Bertha Sommer saw crowds of women and children, some of them leading farm animals. Some of the women carried enamel buckets for suitcases. The roads were stuffed with people fleeing, carrying as many of their belongings as they could, afraid to look back, afraid to think of what they were leaving behind. Bertha was the same, she had also left things behind, things she couldn't carry.

The streets were full of mud too. And full of rumour. The whole of Europe was full of rumour. On the trucks, it became clear that the Russians were trying to close off the escape from the north. The retreating army was trying to make it to Eger on the German border as quickly as possible, but the pace of the streets made it difficult.

On 9 May the Soviet Army had all but caught up with them. The soldiers at the back of the truck spotted them behind. At the edge of a valley, they could see the densely packed road curling through the trees and emerging on the opposite side of the valley behind them. Officer Kern handed Bertha the binoculars and she could see, with great shock, the first Russian tanks and armoured cars in pursuit. Binoculars show exactly how close you can be.

Everybody on the truck began to talk at the same time. Officer Kern silenced them and said the Russians would never catch up. The roads were too clogged. As long as the Germans were not held up somewhere along the road ahead, there was no danger. Besides, there was too much mud everywhere. The tanks could never cross through the fields.

By the time they reached Eger, the following day, they were safe. They abandoned the trucks. It was part of the terms of surrender that all military equipment was to be left behind at the border. The Americans at Eger would not have let them through on trucks either.

The Wehrmacht began to disintegrate. Bertha and Officer Kern got down from the truck and set off on their bikes. The soldiers all laid their weapons down by the side of the road. There were piles of helmets like mounds of skulls. Most of the personnel, like Officer Kern, changed out of their uniforms into civilian clothes. They rolled up their uniforms and placed them under bushes, behind walls, anywhere along the route. A few of them, like Kern, held on to their hand weapons, concealing them among their belongings, just to be safe. Many of them kept their boots. Where would you get boots as good as German army boots?

Officer Kern asked Bertha to drop the title of Officer. From time to time she still involuntarily gave him that prefix as they cycled through Eger. They passed a large refugee camp outside the town on the German side. They saw the American troops who were stationed in Eger and who let the retreating Germans pass freely. There were too many of them to stop.

By the time they reached the foot of the Fichtel mountains, Bertha Sommer knew everything there was to know about mud. It clung to her shoes and to the tyres of her bike. She knew mud in every stage of its composition, how it dried and fell off in lumps from the wheels of prams and carts. She had seen thousands of footprints and wheeltracks.

The sun in May 1945 quickly dried the tracks.

Franz Kern and Bertha Sommer headed for the hills. They were trying to get off the main roads as soon as possible. From now on there were new dangers. Angry Czechs and Poles returning home in the opposite direction. The main roads would be treacherous. There would be thieves. There was nobody you could trust. A bicycle was like gold. In May 1945 it was like owning a ranch. Defending it was like a war in itself, a cold war at least.

They went as far into the Fichtel hills as they could. 'The first German afternoon,' Bertha wrote in her diary when they stopped to rest. It was written in bold handwriting in the evening when they had put sufficient distance between themselves and the main German retreat. They had reached a height from which they could see the traffic crawling along the road. It never stopped; even after 10 in the evening, when darkness fell, the horns and the lights passing along below them went on.

They had stopped because Bertha was exhausted. She had no energy left. She needed to sleep. Here in the first elevation of the Fichtel mountains, they could take a rest knowing that there was less danger of being attacked or getting their bikes stolen. They ate some black bread, sitting with their backs to tree trunks. They also had some chocolate, the remains of their rations, which was meant to last until they got home.

Bertha's arms were burning from the sun and began to feel cool after dark. She shivered and put on her coat. She was glad she had insisted on bringing it, even though it made cycling harder in the heat of the day. She thanked Franz for getting her this far. They sat talking for a while; exchanging biographies.

'Bertha Sommer, born Kempen, four sisters, mother still alive, brought up in a strict Catholic background . . .'

Most of it was already known. They expanded and told stories about themselves.

'Franz Kern, married, no children, born Nuremberg, two brothers killed in action, one a pilot . . .'

Kern hid the bikes under foliage and branches. It took a while. She heard the cracking of twigs and branches. He came back and they talked for a while longer until Bertha began to laugh.

'Nerves,' she explained. But she couldn't stop laughing. She became embarrassed about it. She hadn't laughed like this since she was a child. Since the Third Reich began. She sat by the tree, chuckling behind the palm of her hand like an elated child.

'What's the matter with you, Fräulein Sommer?' he asked.

'It's nothing, I'm just happy,' she said. She went on laughing uncontrollably to herself, excluding him. Maybe it was the cold night air. It could have been fear. People laugh out of fear.

'Halt,' Kern said. 'I hear something.'

She stopped abruptly and fell silent. There was nothing to laugh about. Neither of them said a word. They listened.

After a while, when they were sure it was nothing, she settled down and fell asleep. With Franz Kern, she felt safe enough to sleep. Nothing mattered any more.

Kern stayed awake. An ingrained war mentality. He heard every crack, every microscopic night-time noise on the hillside juxtaposed on to the distant sound of endless traffic along the road below. He had spent the war years listening to radio signals. He only fell asleep just before dawn when the birds set up such a shrill contest of noise that it drowned out every other sound, and every danger.

Somewhere between the night of the 10th and the morning of the 11th of May, all formality was lost between them. They had begun to call each other by first names. Bertha and Franz.

22

Jürgen took me to see his new practice. He had claimed me to himself after dinner while Anke put Alex to bed. It was a duty she enjoyed. It took an hour, often longer, to put Alex to bed. They agreed quite amicably about it. 'You have the whole day tomorrow,' Jürgen said to her.

Jürgen's practice looked more like a reception in an advertising agency than the rooms of a gynaecologist. The reception itself was a jungle with tropical plants and fish-tanks. The fish-tanks came from his father's practice, and Jürgen told me how his father used to scrape the green crust off the glass with a blade every Saturday. He told me how he once saw the blade snap in his father's fingers, and one of the larger fish swam up and swallowed a small shard of it.

Above the reception desk, there was a large, commanding poster of a stork in flight carrying a baby wrapped in swaddling clothes. Elsewhere there were other maternity posters from the fifties and newer posters about AIDS.

Jürgen showed me how the practice was designed with three surgeries, each with well-planned interlinking doors so that he could pass from one to the other, minimizing the time delay between patients. The nurses ran the operation very smoothly, indicating which room was next.

Jürgen and I sat in one of the surgeries talking about his success. I sat in the doctor's seat while Jürgen sat on an examining couch, swinging his legs. He spoke with an infallible doctor's touch.

He told me that he had taken on two assistant gynaecologists. But he was still looking at new ways to make each examination more efficient. They had already ensured that women undergoing examination were in the chair, undressed and waiting under a white towel when the doctor came in. There was a special examining chair in which the woman was hoisted up, legs splayed apart.

Had he become dispassionate about women, I asked. Was it difficult to take his mind off women?

'I don't see women in this surgery – I only see patients.'

He was taken aback by my question, as though I had undermined his professional integrity. But then he understood, everything belonged to the realm of serious inquiry. I began to play with an instrument lying on his desk.

'I talk to them in the third person. I make no connection between their vaginas and their faces. The only comparisons I make are for health reasons. The only thing that arouses my attention or my interest is disease and problems. Actually, the only time I am ever reminded that they are women is with some of my Turkish patients. They will take off all their clothes except the head-dress.'

I was playing with some kind of torch in my hands. I looked at the red light that shone through the gaps in my fingers every time I lit it.

'I examine the prostitutes of Münster as well. It's part of the work I do for the city. My father used to do it too. Every week I examine them and give them disease-free certificates. Without it they can't work.'

It was a while before I realized that the torch in my hand was specifically designed for gynaecological examinations. I put it back and went over to the window. I stood looking down over the square where work on new paving had been abandoned for the weekend. Shallow sandpits into which the paving stones would be placed were cordoned off by red and white tape. A tool shed stood in the middle. A woman waited while her dog on a leash crouched in a sand dune.

'You came at the right time,' Jürgen said.

It became clear that he had brought me here to talk about something else. Perhaps Anke? For a moment, I thought he was going to drag up the past. The crash.

79

'Anke can get very unhappy sometimes,' he said. 'She will do everything for Alex. But things are difficult for her. It's hard for me too, but I understand, because I'm a doctor. I can detach myself from the world, from the emotion. I am used to suppressing emotions.'

'She has gone back to college again?' I asked.

'Yes. She decided that she needed to think about something else. She has to progress. With Alex, she can be so depressed. She has to feel she is going somewhere.'

He came over and stood by the window. There was some premonition in his words. We were both looking out through parallel blinds at the Sunday evening square. There was nobody out there now. I was leaning with my elbow on the window frame. Jürgen's eyes were looking at me.

'Alex is very ill. You know that. He's got leukaemia. He won't live long.'

I expressed shock. Jürgen quickly ran through a medical explanation, giving me the causes, treatment and long-term outlook on leukaemia. There was little hope in Alex's case. I wondered if this was Jürgen's way of protecting himself from his own emotions. When things went wrong, he turned into a doctor.

'It's good to talk to you,' he said. 'Anke and I still find it impossible to discuss it. Together, we still hope it's not true.'

Jürgen pulled me away from the window. He suggested going for a drink. There was nothing more anyone could say about Alex. Nothing I could say to help.

'You know,' Jürgen said. 'If Alex had been born in the Third Reich, he would have been eliminated – life unworthy of life. In ten years' time, his condition will be quite routinely picked up at the embryo stage. I feel lucky for him. Alex is like a refugee. We feel as though we've saved his life. Part of his life, anyway.'

In the lift going back down, I offered more encouragement. Jürgen said they were happier with Alexander than they might ever have been without him.

We walked across the square, finding our way along between

the sandpits and the mounds of new paving stones. We went for a quiet drink on the way home. Anke was already asleep when we arrived back. Jürgen showed me my room, and when I got into bed I found a piece of chocolate cake, half-eaten, under the sheet. At first I thought it was Anke's idea of a little joke. Then I realized it must have been Alexander. It was a gift.

23

The following morning, Alexander was collected by bus to go to his special school. Everybody's life was worked out with sheer precision. Jürgen spent the day at the practice and later in the afternoon went on to the local hospital. Anke normally went to the university, where she had gone back to take up social sciences. That Monday morning she was having a long drawn-out breakfast. She was going to show me around Münster.

She suggested the bikes.

I took Jürgen's bike. I love these German bikes where you can back-pedal to brake. We spent all morning cycling through the cobbled streets.

'What's Münster got?' I shouted after her.

'It's got everything the heart could desire.' She knows how to answer with extreme irony. To say something without irony is leaving yourself open, unprotected.

'Let's see. Münster: it's got a market place. It's got jewellers, cafés, canals, cathedrals . . . and bells, endless bells on a Sunday. It's the rainiest city in Germany. It's flat, it's green, it's got no industry and never had. It's a sanctuary for kite flyers, wanderers, cyclists, and, and, and . . .'

Anke often broke off with the words and, and, and . . . It reminded me of the time we first met in Düsseldorf.

'Is that all?'

'Well . . .' She thought, puffing. 'Münster now has a large concentration of Tommies – British soldiers.'

After another pause she added: 'Münster also has the distinction of being the first civilian target to have been bombed from the air during the war.'

We went for coffee. Anke had strawberry cake. While we were sitting down, she told me how she felt about Alex and his illness. She could not bring herself to say the word leukaemia. Otherwise, she claimed to have come to terms with the inevitable. A few minutes later, quite unprovoked it seemed to me, she started crying. Tears streamed down her face quite openly while she spoke about her life in general. What I found strange was that she didn't seem unhappy. If anything, she wanted to cry.

'I can't let myself cry in the house,' she said.

She talked about Alexander with a false optimism, as though optimism would preserve him from fate. She refused to believe in fate.

'What kills me is all these people who tell me it's God's plan,' she said angrily. 'I get the nuns here telling me I am blessed with the presence of a son like that. All that sanctimonious shit makes me angry . . . All this equality, some day, in heaven.'

Then Anke changed the subject. She was possessed of great diversity, and began to plan out a route for us to cycle. Before we left the café, Anke stole the silver jug from the table, placed it in her pocket and went up to pay the bill.

'Jürgen never lets me steal things like that. He says we can buy all the jugs we want. It's not the same.'

Minutes ago, she was crying. Now she laughed as we cycled away through the medieval streets and out of the town along the red paths; tyres grinding on the sand underneath. We came to a stable in the country, far away from any houses. When Anke saw the owner of the stable, a large woman with a red face, dressed in jodhpurs and riding hat, they greeted each other and Anke stopped. I was introduced to Frau Bohle. We were taken on a tour of the stables. Anke explained that people owned the horses individually and rented the space at the stables.

The woman showed us her favourite horse. Winnitou. I picked an apple from a wheelbarrow full of apples and gave it to a horse called Navajo. The horse gripped the apple with his lips. I watched him catch the fruit with his brown teeth and juggle it around in his mouth as he chewed. To a horse, an apple must be like a piece of chocolate is to us. He crunched for ages. Other horses looked out over the gates. There is something intimate in the way a horse looks at you.

We cycled on. Anke went ahead and I kept looking at the way her feet turned in the pedals. Sometimes she slowed down to remark on something; a feature in the landscape. Then she would race ahead again.

Once a squadron of RAF jets flew overhead reducing the land to white silence. When the soft, grinding sound of the bicycle tyres returned, Anke looked around and said; 'So peaceful out here . . .'

Anke stopped. We left the bikes at the edge of the forest and walked for a while up-hill through the trees. When we seemed close to the top, Anke took my hand and led me out into a clearing where we could suddenly see right across the landscape. The town of Münster was like a toytown on the horizon, covered in a blue-grey cloud, under the streaming rain. We stood together for a while saying nothing.

These were the limits of freedom.

We cycled right into those blue clouds on the way back. It was as though we were travelling to meet them, cycling right into the rain. We got soaked. Anke's hair was plastered down on her skull. Whenever she blinked, dozens of tiny drops jumped from her eyelashes.

24

The change came at last in the Eastern Bloc. The Soviet Union was beginning to collapse. The excitement in Germany about the freedom trains and the influx of East Germans had reached fever-pitch. It was on everybody's mind. On everybody's lips. Quite suddenly, before anyone had time to start fighting for it, the Berlin Wall came down and nobody could believe it. The day of 9 November 1989 was as strange as the day the Wall was built.

This time people around the world were able to see history on television. Crowds flocked to Berlin to chisel away a piece of the Wall for themselves. I watched it on TV myself. I saw the ecstatic faces of women, and men, jumping, embracing each other in the streets, in tears. The ecstasy of history.

Then came Czechoslovakia. I had been there only a month before, and nobody believed it would ever happen. Suddenly the silent power of the majority took over. The small crowds I had seen standing around with candles along the Karls Bridge swelled into thousands on Wenceslas Square. I imagined the deafening sound of all those footsteps in the streets. I heard the sound of keys ringing, the symbol of freedom. Days later, the velvet revolution had liberated Czechoslovakia from communist tyranny. They had discovered the power of harmless masses; and the power of silent feet, and candles.

This time, everybody in Prague was expecting the tanks again. The whole world was waiting for the shooting to start. But weapons had become less than useless against candles. You can't argue with candles.

The streets of Prague were celebrating. People leaping on the bonnets and roofs of cars. Students drinking in the streets. The pubs and cafés were crammed with talkers. Everywhere people were ready to explain, as though they had never done so before, among themselves and to the press reporters around the world. The miracle had to be re-enacted and repeated again and again in words and in smiles to camera. I thought of going back to Prague. Trust me to have visited Prague a month before the greatest revolution in history.

I watched it all on the TV. I saw that the temperature had dropped to freezing point in Prague. You could see people's breath as they talked.

I sent a note to Dr Milan Houdek to congratulate him and his country on their liberation.

Two weeks later, I received a letter from him thanking me. He had checked some of the facts about Louny at the end of the war in 1945. He confirmed them against other sources. He went on to describe the celebrations and the euphoria of the town when the communist government fell. He said he saw people go into the pub U Somolu who had never been inside a bar before. He saw people talking who had never opened their mouths in their lives before. He saw people who wouldn't greet each other in the street dancing together on the square in sub-zero temperatures. At the end of the letter, he wrote this:

You remember I told you in the church that I don't like communists. I could not imagine such great and splendid changes would happen so early. But it could not have been possible without changes in the USSR. Now the communists do not want to leave their castle at Louny, saying it was built for their members. You know the tall red building at the end of the town where I came to meet you? They are holding on to it. We plan to make a people chain around the building. We hope the TV stations will come . . .

I sent a note thanking him for his research. I enclosed some cuttings from British newspapers so that he could compare the reportage. I wanted him to see how interested the outside world was.

Some weeks later, I received another short letter back:

Thank you for your letter. I will write to you what happened after you were here in Louny. The day after you left, two secret policemen came to me. I was asked who you were, where I had met you, what we had been speaking about. They wanted to know if you had a suitcase. They even asked me if I had not made a photograph of you! I had to lend them the books from which you got the information about the year 1945. They were distracted by two things: that you had been inside the communist headquarters and had seen its interior, and also why you had been so interested in the garrison in Louny. Perhaps they thought you was a terrorist or spy. Perhaps they wanted to get me. They had been waiting for the chance to take my job in the archives. So it was with us in Czechoslovakia till 17 November. Now it seems to be a joke, but it was not . . .

. . . Some words about Mrs Sekalova: she visited me. She was too sad and told me her life for communism had no sense. I remembered John Lennon and 'whispered words of wisdom, let it be'.

I sent a further note asking him to let me know what happened to the communist headquarters. Some weeks later I got a note back saying the communists could not be dislodged despite two attempts at a people's chain. I checked his address against an earlier letter and noticed that he had changed his address. He has moved, I thought. Instead of Lenivova 95, he was now at Praska 95. I wrote back and asked him if it was a new address. Maybe he just got rid of Lenin. I then began to realize that they had changed the names of the streets in Louny, just as they did when the Germans moved out in May 1945.

25

It was all behind them now.

Some days later, when Bertha and Franz had put sufficient distance behind them, they felt they could relax the pace a little. They had cycled mostly up-hill. In fact they had spent most of the time on foot, pushing the bikes along. The summer had come into its own. Sometimes they passed a field of rye or a bank of grass exploding with red poppies. And as they climbed higher into the Fichtel hills, they met more and more trees instead of fields. Walking with the bikes was sheer work in the heat. Sweat rolled into Bertha's eyes.

At one point, around noon on another hot day, she was blinded by sweat and banged her foot against the pedal of her bike while walking beside it. She gashed an agonizing cut on her ankle. Bertha dropped her bike, sat down on the grass verge for a moment to hold her leg until the pain slowly receded.

Franz was a patient man. He came back and asked if she was all right. She got up again.

'It's nothing,' she said. 'When I think of what other people must have gone through.'

He held the bike for her. They moved on. She began to forget about her ankle. A thin trickle of blood had rolled down into her shoe and stopped. It became a thin, almost black, line as it dried in the sun.

Sometimes there was a short, swift down-hill ride through a cool forest. A quick spin which made her lightheaded, thinking she could cycle anywhere. By the end of the down-hill run, by the time the road climbed upwards again, she would be almost frozen, with goose pimples bursting through the sunburn on her arms. When she got off the bike, the heat attacked her again.

Once, going down-hill, she swallowed something. An insect.

She tried to spit it out again, veered towards the bank of the road and almost crashed into the ditch.

Franz laughed when she told him. He said she was lucky, he hadn't eaten yet.

They had little food left. Some bread, that's all. They stopped at a farm where a large woman came out and gave them some fresh bread and lard. She explained that she had nothing else left; her store, or what was left of it, had already been emptied by passing refugees heading east. The woman warned about thieves and looters. She made some weak tea with sugar which Bertha and Franz drank by the gate while they ate the thick slices of bread. The woman was leaning out of the window asking them questions when she saw a band of strangers coming down the hill.

'*Polen*,' she whispered, urgently, and disappeared, shutting the window.

The group of men coming towards them along the road were no more than 200 metres away. Bertha and Franz were left with nothing to do but stand and see what would happen. Franz decided to act fast.

'Bring the bikes around to the back of the house,' he ordered.

'But they can see us,' Bertha said. 'It's no use, they'll know.'

'Take the bikes around to the back,' he repeated through his teeth.

She brought the bikes around one by one while Franz stood at the gate, looking at the Polish exiles approaching. Bertha stayed at the back of the house. The tactic worked. Perhaps the passing Poles believed that they belonged to the house. Perhaps they were uninterested. Perhaps they knew they were close to the Czech border and could only hold their home country in mind. Perhaps it was sheer luck.

They passed by without a word.

Afterwards, the woman in the house came out and said she couldn't believe it. She had been raided several times. There was nothing left in the house to take. She had also hidden some valuables. There was no law to protect her now, she said. She was not blaming the returning exiles. It was reparation, she said.

The woman told Bertha and Franz about other people in the area who were less fortunate. Another family not far from there had been terrorized by them and had everything taken. All of their family heirlooms were gone. A woman back in the direction of Eger had been beaten up in her home. Another old man who resisted the plunder had his arms broken.

Bertha felt safe with Franz. She was sure that he was clever and that his presence would eventually get her home. Later on, they met a soldier, a deserter who had spent three weeks in the woods. They gave him directions to get back to Bremen. Franz told him to go over Hof.

From time to time Bertha's mind leaped forward to that moment when she herself would arrive home. She would have to send a message in advance to give them time to prepare for her arrival. Time to welcome her back to life. She had a recurring image of herself on the doorstep with her mother, her aunt, her sisters and the neighbours. Every minute of the journey was bringing her closer.

By evening, they reached a lake, a small lake in the hills. It was a remote place in the Fitchtel hills where the population had thinned out to a few scattered houses. When they saw the lake surrounded by trees, they decided to stop. The sheer beauty of the place made Bertha plead with Franz to stay there for the night. Somehow, the urgency had receded. The race to get home could be postponed. The lake was set in the middle of a forest, far away from habitation. In the middle of nowhere. The middle of Germany.

They felt the peace of the surroundings. They heard those strange lulls in the forest where every bird decides to stop whistling at the same time and then start up again without notice. The sun, still warm, was beginning to sink over the tops of the trees beyond the lake. The insects took over the air.

Bertha wanted to swim. She looked forward to bathing properly for the first time in days and even had a small piece of soap left. It felt like the last piece of soap in Europe. By the time the sun and sky began to tint red, she had found an enclave where she could swim in complete privacy. She had the whole lake to herself.

Franz Kern was a decent man, she could assure herself. She could trust him not to spy on her. He was married. She felt she knew him well enough to trust him.

She removed all her clothes and placed them by a tree. She took only the soap with her. She had felt nothing so free and soothing as lake-water in years. It was so cool at first, it shocked her. Small clouds of soapy water drifted around her as she washed. She ducked her head down and washed her hair. She heard the silence of the lake underneath each time. A silence full of trout.

When she had finished washing, she threw the soap up on to the bank, where she hoped it wouldn't collect grit.

She swam out a little, into the lake. She felt she was swimming with the trout. Her body looked like gold through the brown mountainy water. She had escaped the worst of this war. Even as she was swimming she remembered to thank God; a mental thanks as she turned on her back and kicked her legs. The sound of the splashing echoed across the lake. It was peacetime in Germany. Then at times she had an idle suspicion that Franz might be sneaking a look at her. She dismissed it and thought it was only her imagination. She saw nothing but the interior of the woods, which had now turned dark with the absence of light.

The lake itself was still quite bright. The reddish sunlight had turned the trunks of the trees at the edge to bronze. Bertha swam to the bank and stepped out of the lake, water dripping on to the stones. She left footprints on the hard earth. She began to dry herself, feeling the last of the day's heat. She got dressed and picked up the small bar of soap. With her fingernail she prized off three brown pine needles and wondered if she would offer the soap to Franz. Of course she would.

She threw the towel over her arm and stared out at the lake.

91

The midges still hovered over the water. She couldn't believe her eyes. It was like a painting.

On the far side of the lake, two men in the darkness of the trees had been watching her. Two Polish exiles. They had been in these woods for weeks. They had not seen soap for months. They had not seen the sight of a naked woman for years.

26

When Bertha came back, she offered Franz the soap. He thanked her and went away to wash himself while she prepared the food. There was so little left that it was difficult to call it a meal. They had managed to get some bread and gherkins from a farmer along the way. She was amazed how generous people were towards them.

She prepared the meal as festively as she could. She spread a headscarf out along the floor and placed the food on it. Within minutes, her prepared evening meal had been discovered by ants and she had to rearrange the whole thing somewhere else. She eventually set up her table on top of her bag a little back from the edge of the lake. She had to keep on beating off insects as she did so.

Franz came back. The sky moved through a spectrum of colours until it rested at a deep blue again. They sat down and ate their frugal meal in peace. They watched the blue of the sky fade into a navy. Stars came out. The moon lit up the lake.

Long after their meal, Franz sat back and lit a cigarette while Bertha cleared everything away. His face lit up over the small flame. The red cinder at the top of his cigarette waved about in the dark as he talked. Their voices drifted through the forest and out across the lake. Sometimes Bertha laughed and her laugh would come back in an echo. The red cinder jumped in the air and landed in the lake, where it went out with a fizzle.

They kept talking for a long time in low tones. Franz talked about beauty. He was such a cultured man, Bertha thought to herself. He knew all of the Verdi operas. She didn't believe him at first. But then he sang some notes. He said he was more fond of swing. So was she. He sang the start of some swing tunes.

Sound travels clearly across water. Occasionally, a startled wood pigeon took off out of the trees along the lake. Sometimes they heard the sound of a strange bird. All the time they heard fish in the lake jumping at flies. The mayfly. In the distance, they heard a deer barking. The fervent clatter of nature reassured them. Whenever the woods fell silent, it was almost too empty.

She had been a little disappointed when Franz returned the tiny bar of soap to her with some granules of sand imbedded in one side. But she could forgive that. Otherwise, he was a refined man. Her mother would have been impressed with him. He had nice hands. Maybe it was a pity he was married.

Franz said the forest was like an orchestra of sound. Bertha agreed.

'It's like music,' he said.

'That's true. I was just about to say that myself.'

They could no longer see each other properly in the dark. Only as silhouettes against the lake. It made it easier to say things. She began get her coat ready. Her simple bed.

Franz lit another cigarette. She liked the smell of smoke out in the open. It smelled like the cities she had been in. Paris, Prague, Cologne.

It was late. They looked at the stars for a while.

'Thank God, we're alive,' she said suddenly, almost startling herself. It was something she would only say to herself privately. 'I feel we've been so lucky,' she added, trying to shift the emphasis.

Franz said nothing. Maybe what she'd said had ruined the atmosphere. Why speak about what might have happened? It was so strange being in the dark with a man. But she trusted him. He talked about the stars.

Once again she saw the end of the cigarette being projected in an arc out into the lake, where it died with another short fizzle. Franz approached her and stood in front of her. She could see nothing but the shape of his head against the sky. He leaned forward. Without a word, he kissed her on the mouth.

The calmness of the night had taken her by surprise. She

didn't resist. It would have been like resisting all of nature. It would have felt like denying the lake and all its peaceful beauty. What could be more honest than nature?

He placed his arm around her. At first she gave herself to the kiss, as though she were once more swimming in the lake. She swam in his arms. She tasted the tobacco on his lips. Smelled the smoke in his clothes.

For months during the war, she had renounced all attraction to anyone. Even the smallest liking for anything other than her work and her daily walk to Mass in Laun seemed a desertion of her own principles. Now she had fallen into a deep kiss and realized how much she had liked Franz Kern all along.

What would happen next? She pulled away and asked him to stop.

'Forgive me, Bertha,' he said. 'It's the lake. All this peace in the air. Please forgive me. I shouldn't have done that.'

'It's nothing,' she said.

They stood in soft white light, moonlight reflected up from the lake. She didn't know what to say.

'I'm sorry,' he said. 'It's the moon. I don't know what came over me.'

It was an innocent kiss. What harm, she thought. Maybe he even deserved it for saving her life, for bringing her safely back to Germany. But she couldn't say any of that. She was embarrassed. They said no more about it. They couldn't let it happen again. Bertha began to get busy arranging things. Franz stepped away, down to the edge of the lake, in order to let her prepare her bed for the night. They said goodnight to each other. They tried to behave as though nothing had happened.

The forest was filled with allusions. The lake shone with significance. Franz listened to Bertha breathing, unsure whether she was asleep or not. She lay awake with her eyes open, looking at the stars, listening to the forest. She refused to let herself speak.

27

On the far side of the lake, the two men were still watching. They had seen faces lighting up under the flare of a match. They had heard the voices, and the laughter. They had seen the butt ends of cigarettes being tossed into the lake. Their minds were full of desire. Driven insane by the sight of food, and cigarettes, and the sight of a German woman swimming in the lake at dusk.

All over Germany, the retreat went on, relentless. Everybody in Europe was on the move. Some going home, some going to find new homes. New places where they could find peace. Everywhere, people now discovered the destruction of the war. The Germans were travelling west. The Czechs, Poles, Armenians, among many other races, were all moving east. All those who had been displaced by the Reich and brought to Germany as forced labour were now going back, angry, impatient to see their homes. They took with them what they could carry. People slept by the roadside, under trees, in barns, or under the stars in the fields. Those who had possessions hid them, or slept with them, or held them in their hands, or rolled them up in their jackets as pillows. Truck drivers and car drivers fell asleep at the wheel. Anyone who had salvaged something from this war had a head start on others with nothing. They were envied. They were watched.

And some people didn't sleep at all. They walked on, desperate to find out what happened at home, anxious to restart their lives, longing to reunite with their sweethearts, of whom they still had a small, torn, black and white photograph, or families and children who had grown out of recognition since they had parted. And some people were going home to nothing. Nobody. Just ruins.

There were Polish and Russian exiles who had a long way to go. People who would never even get home. There were men who had escaped from their factories in Nuremberg or Stuttgart and taken to the woods and the mountains, knowing that the war was near the end. Men who had been on the run from the SS and from the inhabitants who would have pointed them out. Men who were angry at the time which had been taken from them by the Reich, who were angry and ready to avenge the stolen years. There were no rules. No code of conduct. It was every man for himself.

The men on the far side of the lake settled down for the night. They had assumed that Bertha was a local girl. After dark, they heard nothing. They saw no more cigarettes lighting up. They assumed she was gone.

They were left listening to the sound of the lake; the fish, the occasional bird winging across the surface. They were tired, like anyone else on the move. They had already raided some houses, ordered the outraged and terrified occupants of remote farm-houses outside while they took with them the smallest, most precious, valuables.

They were aware they had come close to the Czech border. From there on they would have to behave under new laws. Until then, they used the lawless twilight of Germany's defeat. They settled in the post-war chaos and fell asleep.

While all of Germany slept, the chaos of the forests receded. Sometimes an owl broke the silence. Or a frightened dove clattered away across the trees. Fish still broke the surface of the lake where the stars were reflected. Everybody slept. A land that had become used to the noise of sirens and planes was now getting used to the silence.

In the middle of the night, the two men awoke with a fright. They sat up. Perhaps it was already close to dawn. They both heard it at the same time. It was clear. A piercing shout which startled the environment. The sound of it still echoed in their ears like the cry of some unknown animal.

'Did you hear that?' one of them asked.

But they both knew what it was. It was as though every bird and every silent fish in the black lake had heard it too.

It was the shout of a woman.

A piercing cry, somewhere between pain and pleasure. They knew where it came from across the lake. At first it frightened them. Then it filled them with desire and wild excitement; an intimate feeling, as though they were right there with the woman. As though they had participated. As though there was no distance between them and no lake. After that, they began to feel an angry desire. They held their breath, listening for more.

They knew it was her. The German girl across the lake. The woman they had seen swimming. They could still hear the echo of her love-shout receding in the trees, in the widening rings on the surface of the lake.

They couldn't sleep.

28

It was already bright when Bertha woke up. Franz had his arm around her, underneath her neck. She was still half asleep, but she was aware that everything had changed. She looked at Franz beside her, half covered by her russet coat, breathing quietly through his nose. This can't be wrong, she thought to herself. If anything, this was a new start. It was the first day of her life, her new life with Franz. She couldn't wait. One moment she was afraid of what the future would bring. Next minute she was completely unafraid.

She sat up and looked out at the lake. She saw Franz waking up. His eyes and his deep voice banished all fear. They smiled at each other. They talked. They were together.

It was a morning for dreaming. The sun was already beating down on to the lake, throwing a strong white glare back into their eyes. The brightness brought tears to her eyes.

At first, Franz misunderstood. She wasn't sad. On the contrary, she was crying because she was happy. The war was over. She had a life ahead of her. And Franz Kern. The slightest thing would have tossed her into tears. She wasn't worried. She was surprised that nothing worried her. She didn't want to think what her mother would say. All she wanted was to stay on that shore of the lake and not move.

'It's nothing,' she said. 'I'm just happy. Am I allowed to say that?'

'Why not? You're only saying what the sun is already saying.'

Franz said the most perfect things. Nothing old-fashioned, nothing rehearsed. They paused and looked at the water, wincing in the reflected light. He kissed her gently on the lips, on the side of her face, and then drew back.

'America,' he said.

She embraced him. After a long time she slowly let go. Franz stood up and walked to the edge of the water while she sat and looked at his broad back. That was the way they were for a long time, maybe up to ten minutes. He knew she was looking at him. She knew he was thinking about her.

Bertha went to bathe again. She went to the same place where she had been the previous evening. He could hear her splashing and singing. This time he spoke to her, in shouts which echoed back across the lake.

'You're not going to spend all day swimming, are you? We want to get to the USA today . . .'

She laughed. But she felt shy. She still couldn't make herself talk back to him while she was naked in the water. The water was cooler than the night before. She was shocked by it. She was also shocked by the thought that Franz might be so close that he could take a peek at her through the trees. Maybe she half wanted him to look.

If only her sisters could see her now. But then it occurred to her that it was all too illicit and she stepped out of the water again. The soap had shrunk to half its size. She would have to ration it from now on. Who knew when she could bathe like this again?

They had breakfast, what was left of the black bread and the stale cheese. They laughed about it. They ate everything they had. The Breakfast of Lovers. They kept looking each other in the eyes. They talked about America again.

'We'll have to make our way to Hamburg first,' he said.

'But I'll have to go and see my family first. I'll have to tell my sisters and my mother about our plans. And then say goodbye. They probably think I'm lost anyway.'

'Of course,' Franz said. 'We will do this calmly. We're not running away from anyone. We will get married in America, as soon as we arrive.'

'My mother will win back a daughter and lose her again on the same day. But I think they'll all be happy for me.'

There were practical things to think about. Money. She said

she would be able to get some money together. Her aunt would help. And her sisters. They had little, but somehow they would scrape the fare together.

'Two of my older sisters, Frieda and Maria, were meant to emigrate to Brazil. They had it all planned in nineteen forty. They weren't the only ones. Lots of girls and their husbands were going together. But Frieda and Maria didn't go because they fell out with their boyfriends . . .

'Anyway, my mother didn't want to see them go. She would have let them. But she was glad when they didn't.'

'And where are they now?'

'They're married. The eldest is living in Salzburg. Maria is living in Frankfurt. If there's anything left of that city.'

'I'm sure it's like Nuremberg,' Franz said. 'There was little left of it when I saw it last. We were probably the luckiest ones, to be in Laun, in the middle of nowhere.'

Bertha was barefoot. She began to brush off the dried bits of forest debris which had attached themselves to the soles of her feet. She found bits in between her toes. She thought they must have got there in the water.

'You have beautiful feet,' Franz said. It was an honest comment. And it was true. She knew it.

'You think so?' she probed.

'Oh yes. So many women have ugly feet. Real size thirteens. But your feet are so small and pretty.'

She paused. Allowing the compliment to settle.

'How do you know so much about women's feet?' she demanded, smiling.

'No. I didn't mean it that way,' Franz answered. He felt caught out and embarrassed. He didn't want to talk about his wife in Nuremberg. 'I meant, it must be obvious that some people have nice feet. I don't know. All I know is that yours are very pretty.'

Bertha placed her feet on a grass patch where they would stay clean. She bent her knees up and gathered her dress around her legs. With her eyes closed, she placed her chin on the top of her knees, like a child on a window ledge, facing into a wall of bright sunlight. She could feel her hair and her scalp begin to dry in the sun.

'They're not really made for cycling though,' Franz added.

Without opening her eyes to take aim, or taking her chin away from her knees, she smiled and swung out her arm in an attempt to slap him. She missed. Franz pulled back. He caught the arm she had flung out and pulled her down.

Her face was cast into a shadow when he leaned over and kissed her. There was no hurry. The urgency of the past weeks had disappeared too. She lay back on the bank.

He let her go and she straightened herself out again.

'Be careful . . . my hairdo,' she said, joking. Trying to puff up her hair. In moments like that, she reminded herself of her own father's attitude to life. He loved life. He should have had more of it.

Leaning on her elbow, Bertha began to think about a crucial question.

'Franz, what about your wife?' she asked. 'What will you do?'

'I've thought about that,' he said. 'There is no point in pretending. We never suited each other. I don't know if she even wants me to come back now.'

'What will you say to her? You have to let her know.'

'I haven't had a letter from her since Christmas. Maybe . . . Sometimes I think she hasn't survived. Maybe she has fallen victim to the air-raids in Nuremberg.'

'But we have to find out. We can't just leave her waiting for you.'

'No . . .' Franz said. Then he paused to think for a long time.

'What will you say?'

'I don't know, Bertha. I just don't know. I suppose the only thing to do is to tell the truth. I'll just have to try and find her first.'

'But shouldn't you go back to her, Franz? She's your wife, she must be worried about you, waiting for you?'

'No,' he said emphatically. 'I couldn't go back to her. I have felt like this about you for too long. It's too late now, I want to go to America with you . . .

'Maybe I'll send an officer of the Wehrmacht around to tell her that I fell in combat . . .'

29

It was time they left. Bertha shook her coat out; she was ruining the shape of it, using it as a blanket and as a rug. She packed her things slowly. She was humming again. Then she sang what she had been humming:

Hand in Hand gehn wir beide durch das schöne Land,
Und die Sonne lacht hinter uns her . . .

She hummed again as she combed her hair. Everything could be done at such a leisurely pace from now on. The urgency of their lives had gone. The whole panic of their flight out of Czechoslovakia had dissipated.

It took longer than ever to uncover the bikes from their hiding place. And it seemed to take longer to push them back through the forest until they met the road again. When they reached the firm ground of the road, they felt a sadness between them, as though they would never see the lake again.

But you can't go back. Besides, Bertha wanted to keep going, now that she had started this new journey.

They cycled for a while along a flat road which seemed to veer right around the small lake, until they reached the bottom of a steep incline. Though they could no longer see the lake, they were certain they had circled right around it by now. Franz rode ahead. The sun stung their backs. Damp ringlets of hair still bounced around Bertha's neck. At the bottom of the hill, they stopped.

They passed a little farm-house set in off the road and decided to go in and ask for something to drink. They were both so thirsty. Some tea or fresh water, maybe. But as soon as they began to walk in towards the house, they heard a large dog barking at them. There was nobody around. They waited a while at the gate, then decided to leave it. Perhaps the occupants were out.

They moved on, facing into the steep hill. Somehow, it made the speed at which they had travelled up until then seem ridiculous. Bertha felt stronger than ever, but she was actually going slower, lagging behind. She put her head down as she pushed the bike, as though she was examining the patterns on the road moving back beneath her. She heard the dog in the distance behind her, barking furiously, then stopping, then barking a last few times to make sure they were gone.

The incline of the road was so steep that it seemed to go on for ever. Franz said he could see the top and encouraged her. She wanted to stop for a rest, but any time she did so, the bike would start rolling back before she could engage the brakes. Then she discovered that by placing her foot like a wedge under the front wheel, she could stop the bike very well. She would have sat down but didn't want to ask Franz. He was still walking ahead of her, faster than ever, she thought.

She heard the dog begin to bark again behind her, beneath her in the valley. When they had reached a great height, she looked around and found that the lake had come back into sight again. Then she stopped for a good reason; she discovered she had a puncture in the front wheel and called out to Franz.

'What's wrong, Bertha?' he asked. His voice sounded different. A different place on the road, a different echo in the trees.

'It's a flat tyre,' she shouted back. When the echo came back to her, she felt as though the whole world was listening to her.

'Ach, yes.' He laughed. 'That was waiting to happen.'

Franz put his bike down and came back to her with the pump. She smiled and shrugged. He knelt down and began to pump the wheel, but the air seemed to escape almost as fast as he pumped. He checked the tyre for a nail and found nothing.

'You can't cycle on that. We'll have to stop at the next house and repair it. I might need some water.'

He checked to see that he still had the repair kit.

They walked on. At the summit of the hill where the road veered off to the left and down the other side of the hill again, they found a lane leading to another house. From here they could look right back over the lake, and the place on the opposite side where they had spent the night. They could also see the other farm-house in the valley.

'I'll sit down here and look at the lake,' Bertha said. She was exhausted.

Franz began to take off the tyre. He worked quietly, perhaps with a slight rush of vanity, knowing that Bertha was admiring his skill. Bertha sat looking over the lake, knowing that Franz was proud to be repairing her bike. He first tried to find the puncture by feeling for an escape of air. Then he spat over a spot where he suspected the puncture to be. It didn't work. He had to look for water.

'I won't be long,' he said as he began to walk towards the house, hidden in the trees. The small rucksack was still on his back. He came back and kissed her and said he would be back soon.

'Bring back something to drink, if you can,' she said.

Bertha blew him another passionate kiss as he walked away along the lane towards the house.

She placed her elbows on her knees and propped her chin in her hands to look at the lake. She thought she would never be as happy as she was now, and tried to fix that picture of the lake in her memory for ever. The lake looked far more blue from this height. She looked for a name to call the lake. Blue lake of homecoming. She hummed a little. The strong sun was behind her. She could have fallen asleep with the sound of birds, both near and far away. But then she heard a crack in the trees behind her on the other side of the road.

She ignored the noise.

She heard other noises, clear sounds of movement in the trees close by. She heard footsteps coming along the sandy lane, and at first thought it was Franz. She looked around, wincing against the sunlight, and found a man coming towards her.

Perhaps he looked like Franz but less tall. Another man emerged quickly from the trees on the other side.

She stood up. Maybe they were local people, she thought. But there was something wrong. She was certain of that. There was no time to wait and ask. She made eye contact with one of the men. Then she was sure.

She shouted. 'Franz . . . Franz . . .'

She decided to run. Her way to Franz was blocked, so she ran away. She ran down-hill, back down the hill she had just climbed. She heard them running after her. She was faster, she thought. She was getting away, travelling so fast she thought she was on the bike again. When she arrived down at the bottom of the hill, she ran into the trees, just short of the farm-house. She would be safe at the farm. Or maybe she could double back up again to Franz.

The mad notion crossed her mind that it was such a waste to run back down. It was the least of her concerns. She knew she was going to be attacked.

She hid behind a tree for a moment. She watched one of the men arriving on Franz's bike. The other man was on foot, running hard. They didn't seem organized. She knew her dress would give her away in the trees. Again, she thought of trying to make her way back up the hill towards Franz again. Where was he? On second thoughts, she knew her legs would never make it up the hill again.

She ran, knowing that her bright summer dress was shining in the woods. It was getting torn, too. At one point she was jerked back suddenly while running. She heard the fabric strain and rip. She stopped, went back to free herself, and then ran on. This was all wrong. This shouldn't have happened. She wished she had stayed where she was at the top of the hill. Franz would come soon. As she ran away, she had a strange urge to look back and see if one of the men was really Franz. But that was impossible. Her fear was playing on her.

She heard the men shouting after her. The language was foreign to her. It made her run faster. She emerged from the trees into a small field of red poppies. She ran straight through them into a wide farmyard. She kept running across the yard towards the house. But she hadn't gone far when she was set upon by a large brown dog. She couldn't even see the dog's eyes. All she could hear was the bark. She could see the teeth.

Bertha froze with her back against the wall of one of the wooden sheds. She felt all the power go out of her legs. She shook. It was a different kind of fear, she knew. She could do nothing; nothing but try and look invisible. She hardly trusted herself to move her head to look around the farm.

There were a number of things that came into her head right then, quite irrational thoughts. It occurred to her that all this was unleashed upon her life by the encounter with Franz. But she dismissed that. She wanted Franz to be with her now. He would beat off this dog, and the men who were following her.

She thought of more irrelevant things. Apple fritters. She was aware that there was sand in her right shoe and that she would like to have taken it off and shaken it out, standing on one leg for a moment. She was aware of sweat under her arms, a cool trickle running down along the side of her breast. She thought of the fountain in the market square in her home town, Kempen. She imagined that she had no legs, either that, or that she was standing up to her waist in water; floating. She was aware of a farm stench in the yard, something like burning fat in a pan. She was also aware of an increasing population of flies, around her, around the dog, around everything, treating everything as though nothing was happening.

The dog drew breath, pulled back, only to leap forward again with another ferocious stream of barking, coming so close to her that she could smell the stench of its breath. Now and again, she caught a glimpse of the dog's eyes underneath the hair. She felt a cold rush along her back; hair standing up.

When the dog drew its next breath, she asked herself to produce one last act of defiance. Seeing the house at the top of the hill where Franz was, she gave the biggest shout of emergency she had ever heard herself give, almost leaping with it out of the yard and up the top of the hill.

'Franz . . . Down here . . . Franz . . .'

At that moment, the two men came running into the yard. She saw their faces clearly. They saw her, calling up the hill. The dog saw the two men and abandoned her, to attack and bark with renewed ferocity at them. They stopped and walked backwards, pinned back towards outhouses, holding out their hands, concentrating like tight-rope walkers on the dog's upper lip drawn back over its yellowed front teeth.

The men then became aggressive. They shouted at the dog, which only made it worse. It snapped at them. The dog was almost hoarse. And still no occupants came out of the house.

Bertha slipped away.

30

Where was Franz Kern?

There was no reply for a long time at the house he went to. The occupant there, an old man, had at first taken him for one of the marauding bands who had been drifting around the hills since the end of the war. They had already stolen everything from his house and from the house below in the valley.

Franz asked him for a small vessel full of water in order to repair the puncture. The man showed Franz the well outside and then brought him into the house for a moment to get a bucket. The old man was curious. He talked to Franz about the war. He was a little deaf. And while Franz was inside the house, the shouts from Bertha came up from the valley. The old man had heard nothing and registered great surprise when Franz dropped everything to run away.

Franz reached the road and found Bertha gone. He found his own bike gone too. He knew that something was wrong. He called her, and when he got no answer, he was certain she was in trouble.

He panicked. He had no idea where to run at first. Either ahead, along the road, or back down-hill. He saw the bright blue lake, calm as ever. He heard the dog barking below in the valley and made the choice to run down. It was only when he found his own bike hastily discarded in the trees halfway down that he was sure. It seemed as though somebody had stolen the bike and temporarily hidden it among the new trees.

He looked around. He looked up the hill. He called her quietly, thinking that she might be somewhere close by, hiding. He ran aimlessly into the wood. It was only when he heard her shouting again, this time quite clearly from below in the farmyard, that he knew where he was going. He heard the terror in her voice. And he knew so well it was her voice; he would never forget Bertha's voice.

He kept running down through the trees until he came out short of the farm-house. The dog had stopped barking. Franz had to cross a small stream to get on to the path leading to the front of the farm-house. He realized he must have chosen the most difficult place to cross because he had to fight his way through shrubs and bramble. But at least nobody could see him.

He had a soldier's instinct. Instead of calling for her again, he decided to remain silent. The advantage of revealing his own presence to Bertha would be outweighed by the fact that her attackers would know that too. He was talking about an enemy now. He knew there had to be men in the area; he assumed they were Polish or Czech exiles returning home. But he didn't know how many. He imagined four, maybe five. He cursed himself for having left Bertha alone on the road.

Creeping along the side of the path, he approached the farm-house from a concealed point and examined all the windows of the house at first. There was nothing. Some of the windows reflected the sunlight. There was no sound anywhere except the ridiculous sound of birds. For some reason he looked at his watch to see what time it was. It was just past noon. It made him hurry. He edged along the wall and entered the yard. Flies gathered around him in the heat; he was sure they would give him away.

Flies give everything away. Franz realized why the dog had stopped barking. A swarm of flies hovered around a large brown animal stretched out at the side of the yard. The dog might as well have been asleep, but that was impossible. Franz ran over to the dog. A long hay-rake lay beside him. Blood, by now a dark maroon-coloured stream, still flowed slowly along the bright sand, taking it in grain by grain, granule by granule, coagulating. The dog's tongue lay stretched out of his open mouth. It too had collected grains of sand and dust. The fresh wound above the dog's eyes gleamed like a wet, red and brown cloth in the sun.

Franz listened. He heard nothing but water. Somewhere near by there must have been a stream, or a waterfall. Everything around here ran into the lake.

These were some of the irrational things that struck Franz as he turned to look around the farmyard, wondering where to find Bertha. He thought of Nuremberg. He thought of smaller dogs which his aunts kept all their lives. He thought of the noise his Wehrmacht boots would make along the gravel. Better to be in the forest. He had time to think of the fact that he could have just left and gone home on his own. And how crazy it was even to think of leaving her like that. He thought of Bertha, how beautiful she was. He had time to think that all of this was his own fault. He would fight them all, five or six, no matter how many of them there were.

He got ready to run. He wished he knew where he was going.

31

In October 1985, after my first visit to Czechoslovakia, I stopped in Nuremberg, intending to stay for a few days. The reason was to try and find Franz Kern. If he was in Nuremberg, then I would try and speak to him. I had no address, no contact, no lead whatsoever. What I had planned to do was to make a trawl through the telephone directory and see if such a person still existed in Nuremberg.

I stayed in a guest-house on the outskirts of the city. Every day I went into the city, into the city library, a short walk up the hill from the market square. Nuremberg is one of those fine German cities, restored to its original splendour. In the market square I bought the best of apples. I watched the figurines revolve on the outside of the cathedral. I also spotted a pigeon, trapped in protective netting around the many old plaster statues.

The first day, I copied out all the Franz Kerns and F. Kerns that existed in Nuremberg. I was aware that some Franz Kerns might be ex-directory. Then I took in the outer environs of Nuremberg as well. I had accumulated thirty-five Franz or F. Kerns in all. It happens to be a common name in Germany.

I began to phone them one by one, starting with the city of Nuremberg first. I had prepared my questions carefully: I was apologizing profusely for the intrusion, but I was in Nuremberg in search of a Franz Kern who spent the last days of the war in Czechoslovakia, in Laun. If anyone was to ask why I was looking for him, I would say I had an important but private message for him.

I got as far as ten Franz Kerns before I gave up. Each time, I was met with a slight hostility, sometimes incredulity and more often a short *no*. I spoke to a young Franz Kern who had not even been alive in 1945. Most of the people I spoke to were women, older women. Some of them were kind, perhaps quite pleasantly reminded of the past. One Frau Kern told me her husband Friedrich was in France throughout the war until he was injured and brought home. She said he was lucky he was injured, otherwise he wouldn't still be alive. Another Frau Kern said her husband had ended the war in Berlin and spent some time in Russian POW camps. He won't talk about it, she said, remembering that she was talking to a stranger on the phone. She thought I was a reporter.

Finally, what put me off was the phone-call to a Frau Kern who told me that her husband had been in Czechoslovakia, south, near Brno, for a few years but was then sent to the Russian Front in 1944. He never came back. There was a considerable silence on the phone. She was obviously quite old. I felt terrible, dredging up this grotesque past which people had almost come to terms with.

I decided to leave it alone.

I spent a night in the bars around Nuremberg. You can sit quite happily in a German bar and watch people come and go. Sometimes noisy groups take over. You see men sitting on their own. Sometimes you see two women come in on their own. After a while the waitress will remember you and even acknowledge your presence by bringing up a further beer without you asking for it. They were playing Tom Waits a lot at the time. The owners of the bar had stuck a patchwork of cinema posters on the ceiling, among them some old, post-war centrefolds. Occasionally, you could see somebody distracted from the general conversation glancing up at the brown posters.

I got a taxi back to the *Pension* where I was staying. If I'm right, the guest-house was called Edleman. I came to the decision to forget this search for Franz Kern altogether. I didn't like the idea of dragging through Nuremberg for days, asking for 10 *Pfennig* pieces and phoning from yellow phone-boxes to talk to widows who had lost everything. It was cruel.

Besides, I thought it would be extremely unlikely that Franz

Kern would want to speak to me. I was certain he would refuse to reopen the past and explain it to a new generation totally unconnected with the events and unable to understand the way people felt in the war.

I got to my room, my *Zimmer*, and fell asleep. But I never sleep much on alcohol. Soon enough I was awakened again by a familiar creaking noise. The walls were thin. It was coming from behind me. You can't mistake that creaking rhythm of a couple in the room next door. Sometimes it was confirmed by a muffled groan. I sat up, driven by curiosity, maybe excitement, maybe anger?

I heard the pace quicken. It seemed to miss a beat and then picked up with renewed speed, sawing to and fro steadily to a racing counterpoint. I heard the voice of a woman pleading. It occurred to me to bang violently on the wall, to stop them, to interrupt at the most vital moment. I thought of covering my head with a pillow. Then it occurred to me to cheer them on, like a supporter. I did nothing and just sat up, a captive audience.

I heard the woman raise her voice: *Ja . . . ja . . . ja . . .* louder and louder, *Du . . . Du . . .* until it ended with a clear shout of ecstasy. The final rapture shout was a bit over the top, I thought. Maybe she was faking.

Orgasmus-schrei . . .

There was complete silence. I lay back down again. My heart still racing. My eyes open. I could see the white ceiling. I was full of raging desire. Then I felt indifferent. Glad to be alone. Tired. Drunk.

Ready to leave Nuremberg.

32

Jürgen is not a suspicious man by nature.

He couldn't be, if he let Anke and myself cycle around Münster on our own for a day. If he never asked any questions about our crash, then he would hardly start probing now about our cycle tour in the country. When he came home from his practice that evening, he said very little. He asked if we had had a good day. Anke kissed him. But as soon as Jürgen went into the kitchen he found something to complain about. It's often like that; when people raise a small insignificant issue, blowing it completely out of proportion, they must really be getting at something else. Maybe he was suspicious.

He started giving out stink to Anke about the tiny silver jug she had stolen from the café during the day. His tirade could be heard in a sort of elevated whisper from the kitchen where Anke worked to prepare a meal. He had found the jug on the window sill. He knew it was new. It almost seemed as though he knew about it before he got back.

Funny, too, that Anke didn't defend herself at all. As though she was admitting far more than just the jug. By saying nothing, she declared herself guilty to another, under-the-surface, truth. She just hovered around the kitchen avoiding Jürgen's questions. I heard a pepper-mill grinding.

'Jürgen, come on! It's only a jug,' she said.

'But that's just it, Anke. It's not just a jug. I thought we agreed about this?'

Anke didn't reply. She began to increase the volume of kitchen clatter by a small but noticeable margin. Jürgen brooded.

Maybe I wasn't meant to hear all this. I was in the living-room with Alexander, who was pointing at the window, trying to show me something. He kept saying something I couldn't understand – you know the way it is when you try too hard – something like 'Flee, flee.' I nodded repeatedly and kept saying yes, thinking he was just pointing out of the window or at the window, getting excited about nothing. It was a while before I realized he was pointing at a fly going up the side of the window, hidden from my view at first. I stood up and watched the fly with him. Then he was happy.

I lifted him up to look at the fly more closely. Instead of looking at the fly, Alex began to look at my face, examining my ears, nose, hair, without uttering a sound. When I put him down again he began to jump up and down with excitement. Then he ran around in circles.

I felt I was getting closer to Alex. He was getting to know me.

Outside, Anke and Jürgen were still silently battling it out over the jug. She was laying the table for the meal, saying nothing. She asked him to help. He began to open and close the fridge, endlessly appealing for reasons; making up explanations. 'What is this innate urge you have to steal? Is it that you want to remember the café? What is it?' Maybe he had discovered that the jug had become more than a simple ornament to Anke, some kind of symbol or memory of somewhere else, Düsseldorf; events in her life he had not witnessed himself.

Anke reminded him that they had a guest.

Jürgen came in and sat beside me. Alex ran over and threw his arms around his leg. Jürgen took Alexander's face in both hands and kissed him on the head, quietly, regally. Alex did more gymnastics in the centre of the room until he slipped on the edge of the carpet and fell. 'Oooh . . .' he said, and then smiled at us.

I don't know how Jürgen could possibly have known what happened between Anke and myself. I felt he must have followed us around all day, into the woods of Münster. He seemed far too good-humoured all of a sudden. He asked how the day went.

'Fine,' I said. 'That's a lovely bike you have.'

Jürgen raised his palms in a grand gesture of hospitality. It's all yours, he was saying. Any time.

'You shouldn't let her take things like that,' he said, after a pause, bringing up the subject of the jug once again in a more lighthearted way. 'She's a notorious thief. I can't stop her.'

I felt uncomfortable with Jürgen sitting beside me. Again, he began to offer me his boundless hospitality, saying he would teach me hang-gliding; we could go flying, all three of us, or horse-riding – if only I stayed till Saturday.

Jürgen talked about the events in Germany. The news was beginning to speed up. Germany was moving faster than they could print newspapers. Unity was on the way.

'It's an exciting time for Germany,' he said.

What did he mean by that? I began to read things in his mind that were not there.

All evening, Anke and I behaved as though nothing had happened. How can you behave as though nothing has happened? It seemed as though everything was staged, completely rehearsed and unnatural. Every movement seemed deliberate. If I passed the salt to Anke at the table, I had to do it with less enthusiasm than usual. If she offered the bowl of sliced potatoes, she was doing it with general manners, nothing more. If anything, Anke was ignoring me a little too much, leaning a little too much towards Jürgen.

Everything seemed false. Whenever Anke asked me a question, it seemed as though she was not really interested in having it answered, just in showing that I was still a stranger, still a visitor, and still a friend of the family. We were bending over backwards to show the world, Jürgen at least, that we were not lovers, never had been, never would be.

She asked me things I had told her during the day already. She still wanted to appear as though there were things about me she didn't know. A normal interest.

Alexander was the only source of real distraction. While Jürgen fed him slowly, Alex shook his head, sometimes losing or scattering the food which Jürgen had just placed in his mouth.

Jürgen was so patient. He kept telling Alex that shaking his head was impractical. I never saw Jürgen get angry with him. He couldn't. When Alex began to put things on his head, we all laughed out loud together. Alex's blue fork fell off the table.

Then Alex began to look underneath the table. He was making life difficult for Jürgen but easy for us. Jürgen chased him around with a spoon.

It is impossible to hide. And it's impossible to act like nothing happened. You have a need to tell. Maybe Anke thought it was better to come clean and bring it all out in the open.

'On the way home, we were caught in the rain,' Anke said. It gave me a start to hear her say it. 'We got soaked. I've never got so wet in all my life. There was nowhere to shelter, anywhere.'

Jürgen didn't seem to hear her. He was just bending down under the table to pick up Alexander's fork from the floor. Anke looked over at me. She shrugged. I was waiting for Jürgen to come up again and look into my eyes but he seemed to stay down there. Alex went under the table with him.

Anke pursed her lips and sent me a long, glorious kiss across the table. Then she got up to make the coffee.

33

The strain of secrecy makes you want to blow everything; tell all, never mind the consequence. Why conceal what's on your mind? Telling makes you honest.

I have always wanted to ask Anke why she married Jürgen. Why she said nothing to me at the time. I always wanted to tell her how much it killed me. But we never discussed that kind of thing. It was as though any analysis would embroil us in something complicated, something tedious. Anything between Anke and myself has always been simple and short.

Once she got married, I had no wish to interfere. I stayed away from them on purpose. But then I found I had shunned the two best friends I've ever had.

Anke and I had walked off the red sandy path through the trees until we reached a clearing at the top of a low hill. From the summit we could see the flat countryside all around. The town of Münster lay in the distance on the horizon, like a town in the past, under pillows of dark, fast-moving clouds, the sun occasionally breaking through like orange spotlights. Patches of land were lit up. What is it about landscape that makes you think back, beyond your own past into history? Germany looked ancient. I was thinking timber houses, timber fences, horses and carts, troubadours.

As the clouds moved above us, the bright patches of land seemed to shift too. We stood in sunlight, still unusually warm for October, reviewing this shifting landscape. Anke was holding my hand. We could see Münster under rain; the sky and the land were connected by blue-grey beams of rain. Elsewhere, the sun chased the rain. The sky was full of colour.

Anke pulled me towards her, as if to say 'enough of this talking'. I should not have been so surprised; she had no need for an explanation. She kissed. There was something about the shape of her lips, or maybe it's the taste of her lips, that was so clear; I was able to say I remembered Anke's lips. Lips never change.

None of this was intended. Afterwards, it seemed completely unavoidable.

Anke placed the side of her face against my chest. Perhaps I thought she wanted the comfort of a stranger, of an old friend. I kept staring out over her head at Münster under a downpour. Something told me that we would soon be under the same downpour. We ignored it.

These are some of the things that came to mind as Anke took my hand and led me back into the trees. I thought of the evaporation which takes place when the sun hits the road after rain. I thought of Anke in Düsseldorf, her apartment, her balcony. I have never separated her from these memories.

Funny. I began to think of horses. It's happened before. Maybe there is something erotic about horses. The sight of a horse's eye. The smell of horses. The way they walk. The crunch of a horse chewing an apple. I lingered on apples for a moment, apples left on trees long after they ripen, long after the leaves have withered, gone yellow; waiting for the first substantial storm to clear them all.

Anke found a place among the trees where the sun came through. I was aware that Anke had a look in her eyes that bordered on the ferocious. I was aware that she put her back against a tree; you can feel it when somebody can't go back any more.

We said nothing about Jürgen. Would it have made any difference? I thought of Jürgen, working in his practice. I thought of the women putting make-up on before their examination. Then I thought of the bikes badly concealed among the trees at the foot of the hill.

I was aware of the smell of rain. And the smell of pine. I was aware of warmth. I was aware that we were free-standing at times, that I held her thigh with one hand and her neck with the other, that she held on to a branch for support, and that, if anyone had been watching at a distance, they would have seen the top of the tree rocking.

Another squadron of RAF jets flew over the area, not directly over us but somewhere close, maybe two kilometres away, enough to fill the forest with solid noise. We couldn't hear each other. All I saw was Anke's eyes; fierce, in pain, in tears, in ecstasy.

The sound of the jets receded. Either that or it merged with the sound of rain. We might have sheltered in the trees, but we ran down to the bikes and began to set off along the road. The rain bounced on the red sand. There were pools along the path with domes of milky brown bubbles from the force of the rain. An orange spray leaped up from Anke's back wheel. Her hair was washed firm against her skull and in a fringe down over her eyes.

34

Jürgen was bound to have his suspicions. After all, Anke and I had a past together. He had good reason to kill me. I thought of that over the next three days. I had every intention of leaving. Sooner or later, I was sure Jürgen would come back and find us in the apartment, if not actually in bed then both having a shower at a most peculiar time of day: 2 in the afternoon.

It didn't stop.

Anke and I got on so well. We could talk about things. Maybe if we knew that we would spend the rest of our lives together, who knows, we might have run from each other. If I had asked her to divorce Jürgen, she would have said no. But I never asked. If we could have predicted the future, perhaps we would not have have been so desperate.

One morning, after Jürgen had gone to work and Alex had been collected by the special bus, Anke came in with coffee. She got into my bed and we talked for a long time. There seemed no end to the things we had to say to each other. My fear of running out of things to say to people disappeared with Anke.

She sat up in the bed, resting on her elbow, holding her saucer in one hand, the cup in the other, sipping occasionally and letting her head lean over so that her brown, or is it russet, hair hung. I told her that I had been in Nuremberg looking for Franz Kern. I told her what I knew. I explained how I had given up the search back in 1985 and was half-thinking of taking it up again. She encouraged me. Kept saying I should go back to Nuremberg to establish what happened.

It was good to talk to her about it. I told her that it seemed unfair to harass old people who wanted to forget what happened. Nonsense, she said. She would do it herself. But then, Anke never had any second thoughts about anything; she always went ahead applying her first and as usual most accurate instinct. I said it made me feel a bit like a Nazi-hunter. I felt I had no stomach for it, dragging the past out of people wasn't my idea of pleasure.

I changed the subject. I asked her if she and Jürgen would come and see me in Düsseldorf some time.

'Difficult,' she said.

It was stupid to ask. I didn't pursue it. She placed her cup and saucer on my forehead. The coffee was no longer hot, but I could feel warmth conducted through the saucer into my forehead. I could also see that there was still come coffee left. It was glass crockery, the kind that doesn't break when it falls on the floor. She allowed the cup and saucer to balance there on my forehead while I began to laugh, a sort of helpless laugh, knowing that using my hands to remove it or steady it myself was cheating.

'Leave it,' she said, restraining my hands.

The cup rocked with my laughing.

'Handy having you here,' she said. 'Somewhere to put my cup while I'm in bed.'

I struggled to free my hands. I could have remained still and prevented the cup from falling that way. In that case, she said, and began to tickle me. I laughed and struggled with her until the cup tipped over and the luke-warm coffee soaked my chest. She fell backwards laughing while I put away the cup.

Jürgen did find out, as it happens. He rang during the day and said we would all go out to dinner that evening; the last evening. Frau Moltke, an occasional babysitter, came to look after Alex.

At the restaurant, Jürgen pretended he knew nothing. He talked about Germany. And football. He talked about his practice. He was now certain that he would have to employ another gynaecologist, his third. The reputation set up by his father's practice was doubling by the month.

Anke was dressed up. She wore long silver earrings. They looked like lizards. Her hair was tied up at the back. I could see the flame of the candle reflected in her eyes. She wore a tur-quoise off-the-shoulder dress and I could see a sort of matt refulgence on her bare shoulders. Jürgen wore a loose beige jacket with pronounced shoulders. He looked strong.

It was the one thing that I was certain of with Jürgen. Nothing would incite him to impatience. Violence would have been inconceivable. Maybe he was capable of killing for revenge. I wasn't sure. This fine Greek restaurant seemed a good place to take out a gun and shoot your wife's lover.

We spent most of the time talking about Eastern Europe. Jürgen said it was the most important revolution in history. More important than the French Revolution. Perestroika would put us all to shame, he thought. Then he told us about his difficulties in finding another gynaecologist.

'Not a decent gynaecologist to spare between here and Dres-den,' Jürgen said, laughing openly. We had drunk quite a bit of wine.

After dinner, Jürgen ordered coffee and brandy. The associa-tion with the scent of coffee from earlier in the day was renewed. Guilt by scent.

Jürgen spoke up. Quite abruptly, over the brandy, he brought up the subject of Anke and myself as though he had completely forgotten it in the meantime. He hadn't. He was saving it up. First he toasted, then he stared at both me and Anke alternately. Seriously. A little drunk.

'I wanted to talk to you both together about this,' he said. 'I don't want to make it a long drawn-out thing. I know how these things happen. I know the strength of love . . .'

Anke and I looked at each other. We were both completely surprised when it came. It was like an official announcement. I was sure people at the next table were able to hear him. His solemn mood was obvious.

'I will say to you both very honestly what I think,' Jürgen went on. 'I have to say it. I know you are having this affair. I cannot stop it.'

We listened. We had no right to speak.

'I thought, four years ago, when we came to live here in Münster, that it was all over. When you came to visit, I knew you were coming as a friend. This has hurt me very much. I know there is nothing I can do. You will still remain my best friend, no matter what happens. And I will still love Anke, no matter what happens . . .'

Jürgen took my hand. Then he took Anke's hand. It must have looked like a seance. The three of us silent; tears in Jürgen's eyes. Tears in Anke's eyes.

'I love you both so much,' he said, looking from one to the other. 'I have thought about this every minute of the day. It has cost me so much pain, but I would hate to lose you . . . either of you.'

He was drunk. Things got worse. We discussed the whole thing very rationally for a while. Anke made excuses. Something had just snapped inside her, she explained. She put her arms around Jürgen. Her tears mingled with his. I could see that the waiter was making anxious glances. But the Greeks understand this kind of thing. They didn't interfere. They brought more brandy. I've never seen Anke that drunk before.

I told Jürgen ten times over that I was leaving the next day. It was all a big mistake. I vowed to him that I wouldn't do this to him again. Anke looked distressed. She hung with her arms around Jürgen's neck.

And Jürgen put his hand on my throat, with my shirt in his fist.

'I love you . . . you bastard.'

We walked home together, the three of us arm in arm, Jürgen in the middle, stumbling through the *Altstadt* of Münster. Sometimes we stopped and put our heads together in the middle of the street. We passed through an archway where the spotlights shine upwards at the old buildings and past the buildings into the reddish-black sky.

35

I went to Nuremberg.

I began to search for Franz Kern, again, in late November that year. It seemed even more ironic that I should be digging up the end of the war when everybody else was moving so feverishly towards German unity. A new era for Germany. Now it was time at last to drop the Second World War.

I found the old list of Kerns. I had only contacted and ticked off ten Kerns before I gave up. I was surprised at my lack of determination. This time, I would put all discretion aside; I had no intention of being brutal or making old people suffer any more guilt or trauma over the war, but I wanted to know. It was down to sheer curiosity by now.

I booked into a guest-house close to the centre of town this time. *Pension* Sonne, on the fourth floor, no lift; clean, quiet, run by an old woman, Frau Schellinger, and her daughter. It had a phone in the breakfast-room. Frau Schellinger promised to take messages for me if I was out. She told me later that most of the people she catered for were travelling salesmen and American tourists, like myself. I felt I belonged more to the salesman category.

I told Frau Schellinger that I worked in market research. She seemed pleased. Eager to help. She was officially retired now. Her daughter ran the guest-house and she was only really helping out. I rarely saw the daughter.

By day, I made phone-calls and went up the hill to the library. In the evening I made more calls to those who were not replying during the day. There seemed less of a rush. I was going about this in a more strategic way, like a market survey. I enjoyed the task more, crossing off the Kerns, talking to people about the war. I found another Fritz Kern who had been in Czechoslovakia at the end of the war. But the wrong end. He was captured by the Russians near Jihlava. He spent months in Russia before he was released.

I found a Franz Kern who said he had lost both legs in the Crimea during the war. He said he had been loaded on a truck with other dead soldiers, unconscious, taken for dead. He found himself on top of a stinking communal grave when he managed to shout out and was saved.

I went to meet him in a suburb of Nuremberg one afternoon. It took me ages to find his small, one-room apartment. He had a shiny red face and oiled grey hair. Twice a week, Tuesdays and Fridays, he was brought down to the noisy pub on the ground floor of the same building by his son. They would drink beer and schnapps together and play Skat. He had obviously told his story a hundred times over. He was a happy man, with no deep attitude to the war, just glad to be alive.

His son talked about the German football team. His son was very broad, about five times the size of his father. He was able to lift his father and carry him around. The mother had died some years ago. I asked the son his age. He looked at me in a strange way, silent, as though he knew what I was really asking. If he was born since the war, since the legs were blown away. The father answered, slapping his son on the back, saying, 'His mother was a beautiful woman.'

They were the only Kerns I could find who would meet me. Most of the Kerns I phoned grunted suspiciously and said they had nothing to do with the war. There was a particular Frau Kern who didn't know where her husband had been. She dropped the phone and went to ask him. I had this picture of a very old couple, senile, losing all memory, puzzling over the question. It seemed to me that they had lost the memory of the phone ringing, but after a while she did come back and said: *Jugoslawien*.

I wasn't having much success but I was being very patient. In the meantime, I had placed a discreet ad in two German newspapers, the *Frankfurter Allgemeine* and the *Nürnberger*

Nachrichten, leaving a box number. The lady at the reception in the Nuremberg office said that kind of ad was not unusual after the war. She helped me with the wording.

After the phone-calls in the evening, I ticked off the list of Kerns in the breakfast-room, counted the digits I had spent on the phone and went in to pay Frau Schellinger. Occasionally I would see a salesman through the frosted orange glass door, pacing up and down, waiting to use the phone. To phone his wife, I suppose.

I paid Frau Schellinger each evening for the phone-calls. And each evening I would find her sitting in her living-room, or in reception, behind the glass partition. She began to invite me in. I sat down sometimes to talk to her. There was a massive TV in the corner, always on. She talked about reunification.

'The people over there in the East should know that we didn't have it easy either,' she said. She had obviously been thinking about all this, waiting for somebody who would listen.

'You get nothing for nothing,' she went on. 'We all had to work hard for what we have. Every *Pfennig*, we saved.'

Within minutes she had taken out a coffee-table book showing photographs of the old and the completely restored Nuremberg.

'Here, you can see for yourself. Nuremberg had eighty-five per cent bomb damage after the war. Here, there was nothing left standing. Not one house was left with its roof on.'

I glanced dutifully through the post-war black and white photographs of the city. It looked like a village, low walls with rubble. The spires of churches, the buildings I had already become familiar with from walking around the town, were ruins. It was remarkable. The opposite page showed the same buildings completely restored. I knew all this from other German cities, Frankfurt, Berlin, Cologne. But she wanted to tell her story.

'This house had no roof and no floors. Only the stairs were left. We lived here under a canopy for three years. Everywhere, I had buckets collecting the rain. I restored this house with my own two hands.'

I looked around to admire her achievement. It was a fine house in the centre of the city. She owned the third and fourth floors, now worth at least 2 million DM, she estimated.

The TV in the corner was showing particularly explicit love scenes, which she ignored completely. She went on talking about the war. She must have thought it was odd to find somebody who was interested in listening to her.

'If they want some of this economic miracle,' she said, referring once more to the East Germans, 'they'll have to work for it like anyone else. You don't get this *Wohlstand* for nothing.'

The TV was now showing the silhouette of a naked woman standing against a window. I have always wondered how older German people can be so impervious to nudity on the screen and nudity on the front of magazines at the newspaper kiosks. I decided to ask her about her husband.

'He's long dead,' she replied. It looked as though she wanted to leave it at that.

'I'm sorry to hear that,' I said. 'Where did that happen?'

'I don't know,' she said. 'He didn't come back. He left this house to go to the Front in nineteen forty-four. I went to the country, to my aunts. I never heard from him. I came back here after the war but I knew he had fallen somewhere. I never heard anything, God bless him.'

She paused and thought back.

'Sometimes people came to me saying they had seen him. I would invite them in and ask them where, when. I would give them food. Sometimes I gave them money. Or gifts. I was so overjoyed to hear that he was alive, maybe in some POW camp. Other men came and said the same thing. I believed them. My hopes were so high I gave them gifts of silver, anything I had. But then, when the months and the years went by, I realized they had conned me. They had all come just to get their food and gifts. He never came back.'

I began to think of Franz Kern's wife. Perhaps she was left waiting for him after the war, waiting for days and weeks, slowly beginning to believe the agonizing truth that he wasn't coming back. What if Franz Kern never returned to Nuremberg?

I would have been searching aimlessly for him. Maybe I should be looking for him in America.

I returned to Düsseldorf.

I had failed to find Franz Kern. For weeks I was hoping to get some response from the adverts I had placed in the papers. Nothing.

Anke phoned me. She wanted to meet me. She had to meet me. In those weeks, she began to come down Düsseldorf on the train once a week, then twice a week. It doesn't take long from Münster to Düsseldorf. She was back home again by 5 o'clock. We met at the station, we went for lunch. Sometimes we went back to my apartment.

After Christmas, she came down to Düsseldorf regularly, at least once a week. It wasn't just love. She needed to talk to me. Sometimes we did nothing but talk together for hours. Occasionally, we decided to meet on neutral ground, in some other smaller town. Throughout January and February we met in towns like Geldern, Kevelaer and Xanten, where we visited the cathedral. We once went to Kempen, to satisfy my curiosity, and walked around the market square and around the old fountain.

Anke kept telling me how ill Alexander was. He still went to the special school every day. But sometimes she had to take him to hospital for tests. Endless tests. Jürgen was saying there was little hope. Leukaemia was not something they had found a successful treatment for. Sometimes Anke had to postpone our meeting. So we talked on the phone instead. Anke cried a lot. Every time we met she cried for Alexander.

I had already given up any hope of a response from my ads in the newspaper when I got a letter through the box number from the *Frankfurter Allgemeine*. I couldn't believe it. I wanted to ring Anke and tell her. It was a letter on blue paper from a woman named Frau Marianne Jazinski. It didn't say much, just gave the address and a short, hasty note.

'I know the Franz Kern you are looking for.'

36

Franz Kern stood in the middle of the farmyard beside the dead dog. The dog's leg was still twitching, so it seemed. Foam clung to his purple lips and to his teeth. The sun shone directly into the farmyard. A shallow rusted basin full of water reflected the sheen of the sun. Midges or flies hovered over it. This had probably been the dog's drinking bowl, where he lapped the water with his long tongue. The rake with which the dog had been struck lay right beside him. Otherwise the farmyard was empty.

Kern felt helpless. He almost wished he was back in Laun. Again, the unforgiveable idea had entered his mind. What if he just got on his bike and left on his own? It was every man for himself. He could have left all this trouble behind. But the thought was too horrific to imagine. He had to force it out of his mind. There was no question of betraying her. Leaving her to the same fate as this dog. Bertha. He loved her.

He removed the small haversack from his back, took out the hand-gun and discarded the haversack beside one of the wooden farm buildings. He had never used the gun. Only three or four times at target practice. Never in combat. It felt strange in his hand. So easy to carry.

He had no idea where to run. He listened for a moment. He heard water. A stream somewhere. He thought once more of calling Bertha, even just to let her know he was with her. But he decided against it. He made a choice and ran around to the back of the outhouses where the forest began again; two chestnut trees, already in bloom, standing like a gateway into a deeper forest. Surely this is where Bertha ran to. He knew by intuition. There were banks of nettles everywhere else. It was the only way she could run, with bare legs.

In all the years of the war Franz Kern had seen no action. Not that he was looking for it. But he always had an irrational feeling that he was missing something; a phobia maybe that he would always arrive too late. It was a fear he had always had in school, during his tests, when he was asked to read out loud, when he was asked to write on the blackboard. He was afraid of being slow. It only began to disappear after he became a technician, or soon after he was conscripted into the army and discovered that others were slower, less enthusiastic than he was. He had always told himself to do his best. More talented people often did less well, and had less stamina.

Running through the chestnut trees into the cool shade of the forest, he told himself once more to do his best. He was a soldier. He was clever. He would find her.

Up to then, Franz Kern's attitude towards the war had been predominantly escapist. He did at the beginning feel as though something good was happening in Germany, but that quickly faded when he became a radio technician and heard the reaction from outside Germany. All he wanted to do in life was to open a shop and fix radios. At the age of eight, he had put together his first radio, a crystal receiver. With a small ear-phone, he received his first signal like a message, like a vocation from above. He excelled at his trade, working in a radio repair shop in Nuremberg before he was drafted into the army.

His skills were too essential to place him in combat. He became an officer with responsibility for listening to enemy signals. By then he had become familiar with international attitudes on the war. He could understand English, a little Russian and French. His aptitude as a technician saved him from the worst of the war. It did nothing for him now. He felt useless. He felt he wasn't made for action. This wasn't his type of thing. He was doing it only for Bertha.

As he ran through the trees he realized how lucky he was to have held on to his gun. At Eger, when he had taken off his uniform, he had rolled up the gun inside it, but had second thoughts and went back to get it. You never know, he thought to himself at the time.

He was less happy about the boots, which were next to useless now. His feet were baking and the boots made far too much noise on the gravel. Even running along the soft, spongy forest floor, they made a thump which vibrated through the limbs of the trees. They would give him away.

For the first time in his life, Franz Kern turned himself into a soldier. All his faculties were alert. He stopped behind a tree. He closed his mouth to listen.

37

Bertha Sommer remembered something as she ran through the trees. Not something she had time to think about in detail, but a penetrating flash of terror from her childhood. A childhood fear which had never gone away.

When Bertha was seven years old, she had fled from the town warden in Kempen, a man who had repeatedly warned her and her sisters not to play in the fountain on the square in front of their house. The Sommer girls had so much waste paper from their father's stationery shop that they continued to sail paper boats on the water, clogging up the tiers of the fountain and spilling the water over the cobbled square. The furious town warden, who had to roll up his sleeves to unblock the fountain, regularly complained to the Sommer family, often chasing the girls away with his stick, until one day their grandmother let him into the house to teach them a lesson, personally.

The Sommer girls were terrified of him and hid under the stairs, still holding their shoes, which they had hastily picked up, still trying to stop the youngest girl, Gabi, from giving them away with her sobbing. But they were caught. All of them, except for Bertha, who had hidden behind the coat rack instead. They were marched into the front room under the eyes of the warden while Bertha slipped away, out of the house.

It was the most terrifying memory of her childhood. She spent the whole day running through the town, hiding in the park, until evening, when she returned to the house, exhausted and hungry, ready to give herself up.

It was all happening again.

Except that this time she was not running from nothing. This time, she knew what she was running from, even though she had the feeling she would prefer to give herself up. Her legs were stinging her. She must have run through a bank of nettles. There was also that stone in her shoe which she wanted to get rid of. She was close to a stream by the sound of it. Her sense of direction sent her in a wide sweep back in the direction of the farm. Where was Franz, she kept thinking. She wanted to call him. Realized that he was probably looking for her but that neither of them could afford to call each other.

She hid. She moved on. She stopped again and tried to remove the stone from her shoe. When she heard the men approaching, she turned and ran again. They were much closer than she thought; she had actually caught sight of them running, not their faces, but their legs and shoes underneath at ground level. The forest had a visibility of ten metres. Perhaps twenty metres if you looked out at floor level.

Bertha thought of lying down. Instead she ran hard, at first with her foot only half in her shoe, then losing the shoe and carrying it with her in her hand. The men were behind her. She felt an agonizing dart in her leg which stopped her running. They had thrown something at her. She looked down and saw a short pitchfork which had caught her right leg. She fell.

Before she had a chance to stand up again, she felt the pain in her leg. The pitchfork was underneath her. The two men were standing over her. They wore shabby clothes. They were thin. Unshaven. Their eyes had a mixture of fear and hatred. She tried to speak to them, pleading, begging. They didn't answer. They stared at her. She should not have spoken to them. She realized that anything she said in German would only attract collective revenge.

Bertha tried to move away, half attempting to get up. It almost seemed comfortable there, on the floor of the forest. She was too weak to stand. One of the men picked up the pitchfork, almost like an act of courtesy, almost as though they had come to help her up again. She stood up on her own, in defiance. It was only when one of the men grabbed her and kissed her that she pushed him away, with sheer hostility.

She walked backwards. It's never a good idea to walk

backwards. She tripped again on the pitchfork, which had been held out. She lost the shoe out of her hand. It hopped upwards as though she was throwing it away, lightheartedly. She screamed just before she was gripped around the neck. A large hand closed over her mouth. She could smell the hand, a musty, animal smell.

Bertha struggled. Hands invaded her body, all over. But she was overpowered with real shock when she saw a man's sexual organ. The man in front of her had lowered his trousers. It was an erect penis. A dark sac dangling underneath. It was as though she had come across a small, venomous creature in the forest. She could smell it. It filled her with fear.

A hand moved inside her dress. Her breasts fell out of her dress in front. She tried to cover them up again with her hands. As soon as she did that, the hand that seemed to come from nowhere behind her once more began to rush up underneath her dress, between her legs. She had too many vulnerable areas to her body. She possessed too much that men desired. She had the idea that they were dirty hands. She couldn't prevent her dress from being pulled up and her underwear being pulled down. She felt a sudden urge to urinate and couldn't help a small jet escaping.

She felt thick fingers burst into her vagina. She felt the same wet hand squeeze her breast. She felt a man begin to suck at her breast. She felt her nipple in his teeth, smelled the grease in his hair. She felt a sweaty hand around her buttocks; fingers bursting into her anus.

The men spoke eagerly to each other. She was excluded. They discussed what to do with her, in a language she could not understand, shouting commands to each other in low voices. She fell backwards. The handle of the pitchfork was placed on her neck to prevent her from getting up. She began to cry convulsively. Certain that she would not survive; thinking she would never get home again. She thought of her sisters.

Everyone has a duty to preserve their own life, to the last. Even if it seems futile. Every time Bertha resisted, she was hit.

She felt like giving herself up. It felt as though she was caught so badly that she might as well give in. As if it didn't matter any more.

One of the men kicked at her legs until they were spread out. He stood on her shins. The pain was unbelievable. At times she tried to raise her head up to see what was happening, like a desperate patient claiming the right to know. But the pitchfork across her neck prevented it. Her hands were being held almost with a bedside manner.

From there on, Bertha didn't quite follow the order of things. She wasn't sure what happened first or what came after. She felt nothing but fear until she heard an overriding sound fill the whole forest around her; a sound that brought back the whole war all over again. A shot, the clear sound of a gunshot, ripped through the trees, echoing and whistling in her ears. Birds scattered. Wood pigeons and turtledoves flapped away across the top of the forest, like returning distant gunfire.

One of the men fell on top of her. She felt as though her ribs cracked. She was winded and suddenly couldn't breathe. There were shouts, she heard running. The sound of branches being brushed aside and let go again with a whack. The explosion of the gun still whispered around the base of the trees.

The man on top of her heaved and gasped for air. His limbs shuddered, reaching for help. The man kept trying to move, trying to reach, trying to drag himself away from her. It was as though she was choking him. She tried to move away herself, but his weight pinned her down. Finally the man gave three quick bucking movements and died. She felt him go limp. Blood began to flow across her breast.

She felt herself get cold and weak. The blood was warm. She tried to remove the pitchfork from her neck. She sat up and leaned over to get sick, vomiting on the brown carpet of pine needles. Her hair was full of pine needles. It was only now that she felt them.

She heard another shot whip through the stagnant air of the forest. It seemed at once near and far. Only when it faded could she tell how far away it was. It was followed by a further shot, even louder, singeing the air and drowning out the sound of the stream near by. She pulled herself up. Once the sound of the shot faded away, the whisper of the stream took over again. She walked away, backwards. Moving towards the water? She was shivering, trying to pull her clothes together around her before Franz came back.

She was moving away from the body of a dead man. His eyes were open. They seemed to be looking at her feet. She kept moving backwards until she was stopped by a tree.

38

Franz came running through the trees. He saw Bertha, and his crazed eyes raked the surrounding trees. He was holding out the gun. Still a soldier.

'Where are they?' he shouted. 'The others, Bertha, where are they?'

'No, Franz, there were only two,' she said.

Bertha was as much afraid of him at that moment, until Franz relaxed his grip on the gun and went over to her. He placed his arms around her and held her very close, with the gun still in his hand.

'It's all right, Bertha. Bertha, *mein Schatz*. It's all right. I'm here now. I'm here with you now.'

Franz kept on repeating the words, comforting her with his best phrases. She began to cry properly now. It was release. She tried to talk through her tears, but he spoke for her.

'It's all right. Don't speak about it now. Let's go. Let's leave all this behind.'

He kissed her again and again. He kissed her crying eyes and stroked her hair. He moved his head back and smiled at her.

'Look, Bertha, I'm here with you now. You have nothing to worry about now. It's all over now. Come on, let's go.'

He held her chin in his hand gently and extracted a tiny smile, as though from a crying child. He pulled her towards himself again. His shirt had taken up some of the blood from her clothes. He led her away towards the stream.

At first Bertha felt only glad to be alive, glad to be safe. The fear she had experienced had numbed her whole personality, so much that she did everything with an automated sense of precision. Fear turns people into machines.

At the small stream, Bertha first knelt down to pray. It gave her the strength to go into the water and wash herself, to forget what happened and to carry on. All of this is God's will, she told herself. The sun lit up the brown flowing water all around her. The water made her feel strong. Her hands splashed the water upwards, mechanically.

Franz stood on the bank with his back to her, allowing her to wash in privacy. It restored her dignity. He still had the gun in his hand. He still scanned the surroundings for signs of attack.

Bertha began to feel the security of Franz's presence. She felt human again. Her courage came back. She would have to forget what happened. She was still in great shock. But she told herself to put it all behind her. She began to feel clean again.

Franz helped her to step out of the stream and placed his arm around her.

'Bertha, *mein Schatz*,' he kept repeating as he led her away. 'What did they do to you? Are you all right?'

'Yes, Franz. I'm so glad you're here.'

She had no injuries. She was alive. She was safe. But then the reality broke in on her.

'What have we done, Franz?' she asked, looking in the direction of the dead body. The fear she had felt earlier had now turned into a heightened sense of guilt. The feeling of total security made her lightheaded with compassion. 'Franz, we have killed somebody here,' she said.

Franz was shocked that Bertha could feel anything for her attackers. He stood in disbelief, almost in anger, when she stopped to look around once more at the man lying face down on the ground. As though she wanted to see the expression on his face, to see who had died on her behalf.

'My God, Franz, what have we done here? Is he dead? Are they both dead?'

'Yes, Bertha. Don't think about it. There was no way out. They would have killed you. And me. We had no choice.'

'Where did you get the gun?' she asked, as though it all had to be made clear in her mind before she could leave. 'I thought you left it in Eger.'

'Lucky I didn't,' he said.

She pulled herself towards him. Little by little, they both realized that they had extended the war.

'We must get out of here,' Franz urged.

It sounded like a military command. She went back to the corpse with him to find her shoes. They were in two different places. The second shoe was right beside the dead man. Franz picked it up for her. She didn't want to look, but she couldn't help glancing down at the man who had threatened her own life so recently. Secretly, she knew that seeing him dead was a comfort. The blood had seeped into the dry brown pine needles. The man's eyes stayed open. Ants had begun to claim his head, running across his oily hair, ears and face. As she put on her shoes, Bertha guessed how old the man must have been; no more than twenty-five, maybe thirty: no older than Franz.

Once the threat to herself had disappeared, Bertha began to feel the strangeness of rational thought. She wanted to talk about it. She wanted Franz to keep telling her it was over.

Franz pulled her away and led her quickly through the wood back towards the farm. There, Bertha got another shock when she saw the dead dog lying motionless in the yard. She realized then exactly how close to death she had come.

Franz picked up his haversack and pulled Bertha along by the hand. It was as though she was reluctant to leave. As though she wanted to let everything sink into her memory at a slow pace. This had all happened too fast for her. Too shocking to remember.

Everything was rushed from there on. Franz said it was getting late. They walked up the hill again. Bertha thought it must have been hours ago that they had started off from the lake. When they reached the top, they decided not to say anything to the old man in the house. They stopped only long enough for Franz to fix the puncture. Bertha was thirsty and wanted a drink of water from the well. Before she went in, she put on a new dress, discreetly, behind a tree. It was the navy blue pleated dress, not exactly the right thing for cycling or for the summer.

It was really more of a winter dress, bought in Paris. But it was just the thing to put the ordeal behind her.

The old man gave her some tea. He also gave them some bread and jam, proudly telling them that the jam was from 1943. He had a hearty laugh and Bertha felt how strange it was to be back among ordinary people again. She began to feel at home and talked to the old man about various things. Irrelevant things, it seemed to her. She accepted a jar of jam which the old man offered her. It was for their journey, the old man insisted. She remarked on the extraordinary kindness as she gave it to Franz to put in his haversack.

They told the old man nothing of what happened. It would have been unfair to burden him with these details. The poor old man wouldn't be able to sleep at night, thinking about the bodies in the forest. They kept the nightmare to themselves.

It was late afternoon by the time they left to resume their journey. Once more, there was a sense of urgency. They had to get away from the area by nightfall. When they rejoined the road on their bikes, Bertha took one more look at the lake. It looked just the same as it did the day before. A deep blue unbroken surface. For a blind moment, they stopped the bikes and stared, wishing they could erase the day and start all over again from the beginning.

They freewheeled down the hill into the next valley. At the bottom, Bertha asked Franz to stop so that she could throw away the dress she had been wearing earlier. It was torn and stained with blood. It could have been washed and mended, but she was anxious to discard any association with that day.

'I want to forget that anything happened,' she said, looking into his eyes.

'Yes, Bertha. We will say nothing about it. Ever.'

'We'll put it all behind us. When we get to America, it will be only a tiny thing in the past.'

She rolled up the dress with a hint of courageous ceremony. Before she went to the ditch along the road, she stopped and turned around again.

'Do you want to put the gun in as well?'

Franz looked at her. He was reluctant. He thought for a moment, as though the forests were full of enemies. But then he agreed. He placed it in the dress she held out with both hands. Bertha rolled it up and concealed it under a bush.

They cycled on through the evening, for almost seven hours without stopping. Without talking. Without remembering. By the time they got to Bayreuth, it was already dark. Bertha was exhausted. Hungry. Still frightened, but safe. They felt the comfort of reaching such a civilized and cultured town. Wagner's town. Drowned in culture and peace.

39

Anke and I kept meeting. Almost every Wednesday, she either came down to Düsseldorf or else we met somewhere else along the way. Sometimes we had lunch and just talked for an hour or two before we parted at the train station again. She had less and less time because of Alex. She was always anxious to get back and pick him up early from the school. He was getting worse.

Once she brought Alex with her, though he was clearly unwell. She thought Alex might enjoy the train journey, it might make him glad. It wasn't a long trip, only as far as Gelsenkirchen. I was there to meet them. Nothing of what Anke had told me in the past weeks had prepared me for the shock of seeing him arriving in a wheelchair, so weak and thin. He was listless. All his energy had disappeared. I could see he was dying.

He didn't recognize me. He wouldn't respond to anything I said.

'You shouldn't have brought him,' I said, when we sat down in a café close to the station. 'I'm sure it's too much for him.'

'I thought the train would make him happy,' she repeated, stroking Alex on the head. 'I thought he would like to see you.'

Alex wouldn't eat anything. He had lost interest in cake, juice, everything. He just sat in his wheelchair, rocking his head from side to side, looking up at his mother. His tongue had gone slack and kept falling out of his mouth. His eyes were red. He didn't know who I was. He just sang, or moaned, or hummed, with his tongue dribbling saliva down his chin. He stared and ignored the clatter all around him in the restaurant.

Anke couldn't stay long, obviously. I'd have liked to have taken them somewhere, maybe shown Alex some things, but he wasn't seeing anything. He didn't know where he was. And

Anke talked urgently about Jürgen, how things had become unbearable at times in the house. They were having these arguments late at night.

'Does he know you come down here to meet me?' I asked.

'I don't know. Maybe he does. He's never said anything.'

'Maybe he's suspicious. Maybe he has followed you once.'

'Maybe,' she said, dismissing it. 'I don't think that really is the problem . . .

'It's Alex,' she whispered. She leaned across the table and explained that Jürgen had rejected any active treatment for Alex's illness. It was terminal. 'So now Jürgen is talking about euthanasia. He has nothing against it. He's positive about it. But I'm not.'

'But what does he suggest?'

'I don't know. He explained it to me, but I couldn't give you the details. My attitude is that Alex should be given a chance, no matter what it costs. No matter how hard it is on us.'

Anke was clearly upset, whispering to me like this. It was breaking one of her closest principles to talk about Alex while he was present. I asked her more questions. I had dozens of things to ask, but Anke stopped talking.

'I'll phone you and talk about it,' she said.

Then she had to bring Alex to the wash-room. That took a long time, almost half an hour, while I sat in the café thinking. I wished there was something I could do for Alex. I wished there was something I could say that would make him smile, just once.

When they came back, I tried to speak to him, but he didn't respond. I could think of nothing that might draw him out.

I looked at Anke. I think it was the only time I met her on these visits that she refused to cry. She wouldn't allow herself to cry with Alex there. It was only alone with me that she could properly grieve about her life.

We talked for a while about Jürgen's practice. She told me that Jürgen had finally employed another gynaecologist. She would have to be careful now, because Jürgen had more time on his hands. But he was still spending all of his day either in the practice or with Alexander. His energy was boundless.

Anke told me that she and Jürgen still slept together. She still loved Jürgen. Nothing had changed in that respect. And he still loved her. If he knew anything about our weekly meetings, he was accepting it. Maybe he had begun to accept, as I did, that Anke could never be tied down. She thrived on freedom.

She began to tell me about the afternoon when Jürgen came home early from the practice and forced her to make love. She had not rejected him or asked him to stop. But he had forced himself on her like a stranger.

I asked her if it was repulsive to her.

'It wasn't that,' she whispered, leaning over the table again, whispering. 'It was the way he did it.'

She was reluctant to talk while Alex was there, sitting so passively beside her. Then she felt she had to say it.

'You know what he did? He raped me. There is no other word for it,' she said. 'I think he really wanted it to be like that. He didn't ask me. He could have asked me and there would have been no problem. But instead he came bursting in and dragged me into the living-room by my hair and then threw me on the floor.'

Anke looked around the restaurant as though she was afraid somebody might be listening.

'He didn't talk. He didn't kiss me or fondle me or anything, he just brutally raped me. He wanted it to be like that. He wanted to act like a complete stranger.'

'But how?' I asked. 'Did you resist or something? Did you try and stop him?'

'No, no,' she insisted. 'I would never do that. Maybe I would play hard to get. But he knows that. No . . . this time he had obviously made up his mind to rape me. I don't know where he got the idea, maybe at the practice . . .

'He just threw me face down on the floor and said: I'm going to fuck you.'

She was fingering one of the silver milk jugs on the table,

perhaps thinking about putting it in her pocket. But she was concentrating on Jürgen.

'It was anal . . .' she whispered. 'He buggered me.'

For a moment, we both paid more attention to our coffee than to anything else. Anke looked around the restaurant to see if anyone was watching her.

'I still can't walk,' she said, smiling. Then she seemed to change her attitude towards the whole episode.

'It's not as though I'm against it, or anything like that. It's just the manner in which he did it. He wanted to frighten me. Afterwards, he was very sorry. He kept saying how sorry he was. He kept hugging me and saying he would never do it again.'

Alexander was staring at some people at the table next to us. They seemed irritated by it. Perhaps they were put off their food.

'He's been apologizing for it ever since,' Anke said after a pause. 'I think he really was very sorry about it. He keeps saying he doesn't know what came over him. It was so unlike him. I tell him to forget about it, but he can't. He keeps telling me how much he regrets what happened.'

It was time for Anke to leave again. She would phone me, she promised. I took them to the station. On the way, we talked about other things. I told Anke that I had received a letter from somebody who had known or who knew where Franz Kern was. I told her I would be going back down to Nuremberg soon.

I walked on to the platform with them. I made sure they got on the train all right and waved at them when the train began to pull out. Alex didn't move. Anke took his hand and waved it for him. It was the last time I saw him.

Then I got my own train back to Düsseldorf. I couldn't stop seeing this image of Alex, waving. I had this imaginary view from the air of two trains speeding away from each other in opposite directions, Anke and Alex on one, myself on the other, all of us staring out at the fields, at the flat landscape of the Ruhr valley.

40

For weeks, Anke had stayed at home every day with Alexander. I told her it would be better for her not to come down to Düsseldorf any more until Alex was better. She said he wasn't going to get better. Anke was on the phone to me almost every day to give me the details. She was sick with sadness. Jürgen had been putting forward his proposal again to give Alex a peaceful, premature death. They couldn't bear to see him suffering any more.

Anke was unsure about the idea. I could see that she had second thoughts; stronger feelings of doubt and guilt. She kept asking me what to do. I told her it was unfair for me to influence her one way or the other. It was so easy for me to say something on the phone.

The next day she rang up and said she was coming to Düsseldorf the following day. She needed to discuss the whole thing; she was racked by indecision and Jürgen was placing her under pressure. The nurse would look after Alex. She dismissed any danger of Jürgen arriving home unexpectedly and counting the hours she was away. She insisted she had to meet me. I agreed to meet her at Düsseldorf station this time, on the Intercity arriving at 11.

I left the apartment early the next morning. It plagued me to think of Alexander. Somehow it seemed that Anke wanted my consent. My blessing. All I had to say to Anke was, yes, Anke, I believe you're doing the right thing, and it would be over. Why would she not leave me out of this?

By 10.30 on Wednesday I stood waiting for her in the underground aisle of the *Hauptbahnhof*, walking up and down, past the flowersellers, the bookshop, the magazine shop, every now and again passing the escalator to platform 13, from where she would emerge. I had waited there so often for her to spring into view suddenly at the top of the escalator. Lately, there was a distraught look in her eyes; even though she smiled, I could see she was thinking back to Münster and her son.

I heard the announcements spilling down from the platforms. The Intercity from Osnabrück and Münster arrived. Passengers came rushing down. I kept searching the faces for Anke's. Ready to embrace her and lead her away. But she wasn't there. Instead, almost the last passenger to come down the escalator, I saw Jürgen.

'Jesus,' I said, almost out loud.

My first impulse was to run, or to hide. I thought it was some coincidence. But then Jürgen had seen me. He came down with his hands in his pockets, smiling. Then he extended his arms towards me. He embraced me, his hands clapping my back. He had a tearful expression.

'I am glad to see you. It's been so long.'

I couldn't believe this was true. I might have expected him to show only resentment and hostility at this stage. I was taking Anke away from him. I might have expected Jürgen to kill me, maybe to plunge some gynaecological instrument straight into my back. Instead I felt the warmth of his friendship.

'I came instead of Anke. She stayed at home with Alex. We are very worried about him.'

He led me away with his arm around my shoulder. I kept asking myself questions. Why didn't Anke phone and warn me? Maybe she did. Then Jürgen answered for me.

'Anke tried to phone you, but you were out.'

Jürgen was wearing a suit. It looked as though he had taken his white coat off and come straight from the surgery.

'How is Alex?' I asked.

'That's what I've come to talk to you about,' Jürgen said. 'I'm not going to talk about you and Anke. I know that you meet. But I haven't come here to talk about that. There is not much I can say anyway . . .

'I've come to talk to you as a friend. Can we go somewhere for lunch around here?'

I suggested an Italian place close by, where I had intended to bring Anke. It felt so strange to be walking with Jürgen. I was still getting over the fright. But I was glad to talk to him. I had missed him.

'Has Anke told you?' he asked.

'Yes. About Alex, you mean?'

Jürgen knew the restaurant. He could have looked around and thought to himself: so this is where they meet. He could have run a hostile imagination over the Italian décor, over the menu, over the waiters and the stone busts which were placed all around, at the doors and at the wine bar. Instead, he showed none of that. It was as though he had a deeper imagination. As though Anke and I were only on the surface, or as though he understood what we did without malice.

The waiter took the order for cannelloni and brought wine. Jürgen sipped the wine calmly and began to talk. He leaned forward towards me.

'I've come here because I want to ask you something. I want your advice. You know that I am going to go ahead with this act of mercy for Alex. We cannot bear to see him suffer any longer like this. You have met him yourself. What would you do?'

I was surprised, both by the direct question and by the fact that he knew so much about Anke and myself; even about Alex's trip to Gelsenkirchen. I had thought about my answer. It was the same as what I would have said to Anke.

'I know you're not doing it for yourselves,' I said. 'I know you are doing it for Alex. It kills me to hear it. I thought he looked terrible when I met him. Maybe it is for the best. But I don't know the medical background. I don't know what his chances are. But if his life has become as pointless as you say, then I am behind you.'

'He has no chance,' Jürgen said, looking down at the table.

Jürgen began to explain the whole background to me. He did it like a doctor, without any emotion, without any hint of

151

personal attachment. He weighed everything up and made it very clear; basically it was all down-hill for Alex. There was no hope for leukaemia cases like this. Then he began to explain his plan to spare him the pain of slow death.

'It's easy for me to talk about it, as a medical expert. It detaches me from the real tragedy,' he said. 'I am driven only by the urge to cut short his agony.'

'But how are you going to do it?' I wanted to know.

'It is very simple. It's done on the drip, you know, intravenously through the arm. First sugar, then pain-killers, morphine, then potassium. It could be done with morphine alone at this stage. But that is the best way. Basically, Alex will just fall asleep.'

Jürgen said it all without enthusiasm, as though he couldn't stomach the idea himself. He hated the efficiency of his plan, but saw no way out.

'Of course, the whole thing is very risky for me. If this is discovered, my life is finished as a gynaecologist. I have thought about all of this. If somebody found out, or exposed me to the public, I would become a household name, for the wrong thing. The press would seize on something like this . . .

'But I don't care. I want to do this for Alex. There is no way out.'

There was no way that anything I would say was going to stop him. I trusted him. I told him it wasn't my decision, but that I was fully behind him. I didn't want him to risk his profession. I told him I was on his side.

'I don't know when exactly it will have to be done. I will phone you. Or Anke will phone you.'

We walked back to the station, up to platform 13 for the Intercity to Münster. Jürgen said that after all this was over I would have to come and visit them again. He would definitely take the time off to teach me hang-gliding.

41

Three weeks later, I was on my way to Nuremberg again to meet the real Franz Kern. The woman, Frau Jazinski, who had answered my ad in the *Frankfurter Allgemeine*, tried at first to establish my reasons for wanting to meet him. She wouldn't even say whether he was alive or not. She asked me to give my reasons in writing in the most specific terms. I remained evasive in my next letter, stressing that I had nothing to do with researching war crimes or anything. All I wanted was to pass on a message from somebody, a colleague who had been in Laun with Franz Kern.

Eventually, Frau Jazinski gave me a cautious invitation. I phoned her and set up a date to travel to Nuremberg. She still gave little information about Kern, and I had the feeling that she was acting as a go-between, that it was really Franz Kern who had seen the ad and asked her to vet me on his behalf.

I stayed at the *Pension* Sonne again.

'Another market survey?' the owner Frau Schellinger asked with a broad smile. She told me straight out that she liked it when her old guests came back again.

The following afternoon I went to visit Frau Jazinski at the address she had given me, a large house close to the city centre. She answered the door herself and searched me with her eyes. I could see she had her suspicions about me. She turned out to be Franz Kern's daughter, his only child. She offered me some coffee and told me that her father had just recently come out of hospital and that he was still unwell. With that, she asked me to give the message to her so that she could pass it on to him.

I told her it was personal. I could only pass it on myself. All this was beginning to sound far too clandestine and intriguing. I wished she weren't so suspicious and that everything would be more simple. I assured her again that I had nothing to do with war-crimes detection. I had no interest in the holocaust. I would leave that to somebody with a clean slate.

By the time she agreed to drive me over to her father's apartment I realized that she had been kept completely in the dark. She wanted to find out something for herself before I met Kern. He had told her nothing about Laun. And nothing about the journey home either.

On the way over in the car, Frau Jazinski became more friendly. She began to tell me about their business. They owned a big hi-fi shop in the city centre. She insisted on driving down the street and asking me to look at the shop.

'My father started this business on his own after the war. It wasn't easy. Things were very hard for him and my mother. They had to save every *Pfennig*.'

How often had I heard that story? She went on praising her father for building up the shop. In the past ten years, with her husband taking over as managing director, the turnover had multiplied a hundredfold, she said proudly. I told her she was in the right business.

She still didn't know exactly why I had come to visit her father. Franz Kern had consented to see me without telling her why. She was sure it would all come out sooner or later.

I asked her about her mother. She was dead. Almost ten years ago.

Franz Kern lived in the top half of a house. The living-room had a spacious balcony looking out over a large garden. The walls were lined with books. The place was well looked-after.

I was going to be surprised by this meeting. I had no idea what he looked like, no idea what to expect.

Franz Kern was a tall man; even in his late seventies, he was as tall as I was. He stood up from his chair by the window to greet me, grimacing a little with stiffness or pain. I begged him not to get up on my account. We shook hands and he asked me to sit down, pointing with the palm of his hand towards an armchair. He was a very calm man, who moved around the room slowly on his stick. He was able to close the window on his own, until his daughter came running and told him to leave it to her. Maria, as he called her, went out to make coffee in the kitchen.

Kern looked at me for a long time. He had a likeable smile. You could have nothing against him. He just kept staring at me until I looked away. Old people are allowed to do that.

'You look like her,' he said quietly.

I didn't reply.

'Bertha ... Where did she get to?' he asked, almost in a dreamy way, still looking at me, but somehow as though he was actually talking to her. And somehow, he wasn't expecting me to answer. He put his finger up to his mouth to say: Shhhh.

He didn't want his daughter to know. We sat like mute men looking at each other while Maria brought in the coffee, filled the cups and apportioned the ostentatious strawberry cake she had brought. We sat there without ever mentioning anything. Kern was saying nothing while Maria was there. So we talked about the united Germany – what else? It was like talking about the weather. Maria said how exciting it was for Germany. Kern sat back.

'At long last,' he said. 'At last, we can breathe like Germans again. It's what we were all running from at the end of the war. This Soviet monster . . .'

He seemed angry.

'We saw the tanks, the Red Army tanks behind us as we fled . . .'

He wasn't boastful; I've met survivors with varying emotions, from anger to indifference. I've met survivors who talked about their luck, like a lottery prize. And survivors who claimed credit for their own lives, people who reckoned they were indestructible, as though they had an invincible charm which saved their own necks. They made themselves look like those trick birthday candles which flare up every time you blow them out. It was as if nothing in the perverse logic of the Reich had anything to do with it; their being alive. There were others I met who had put their trust in God, and thanked God with every mouthful of cake, with every word, for their existence.

Franz Kern was none of these. He acknowledged that he was just lucky, no more. Or can you say that survivors are lucky, he asked. Can you be lucky at the expense of somebody else? In any case, Kern didn't take his life for granted.

He turned to Maria, his daughter, and asked her if she had something to do in the area. If she wished, she could leave us to talk for a while. She was a little put out. But she left and said she would be back in an hour. I told her I could make my own way back if she liked. But she insisted on driving me back. She was afraid her father might never tell her anything and was determined to squeeze some information out of me on the way home.

'I've thought a lot about luck,' he said, as soon as Maria was gone.

'I think we gave too much credit to luck, after the war. It really was made out to be something. We tried to make certain that we could make it a permanent thing; everyone worked hard to ensure that luck was stacked up for themselves. I mean, why should anyone have to be lucky to be alive?

'Then they try to pass the luck on to their next of kin.'

He nodded at the door where Maria had gone out. He included himself in all his observations. He spoke freely, as though he had often spoken to me before, or as though he had been waiting for years to say this to me.

'Idiots. Today we take luck for granted, here in Germany, and we don't know what to do with it. I have never seen Germans so unhappy. This business with the Wall and German unity is not going to make them happier either. I see my own daughter, Maria, strangled by luck.'

Kern stopped talking and looked at me again for a long time, as though he hadn't seen me for years.

I had come to ask him questions. I wanted to know about Bertha Sommer. What happened? He was going to tell me everything, honestly. Otherwise he wouldn't have asked me to come. I knew he would unfold everything in his own way; he had nothing to hide. And there was no need to force anything.

I told him how the diaries of Bertha Sommer had come into my hands and how they ended abruptly after the war, in May 1945. She had taken them up again, years later, but they had become domestic, they talked about happy moments in her life, the linguistic charms of her children when they were small, locks of hair etc. But there were five attempts to write down what she called 'something very painful'. Some agonizing memory which she could never get rid of or share with anyone. She had written it to her own children, a letter which was not to be opened until after her death, in which she wanted to unfold a 'heavy secret'. But she never finished it. After a while she must have learned to suppress it.

'When did she die?' he asked, sitting up suddenly.

'August the sixth, five years ago,' I said.

'I'm sorry.' He stared at the floor for a while. 'I never found out where she went. Where did she go?'

'Vermont,' I said. 'She spent all of her life in America, living in Vermont. As far as I know, she came back to Germany once in the sixties, that was all.'

Franz Kern became even more silent and pensive.

'So she got to America after all . . .'

I realized that Kern needed long pauses of silence to assimilate the information and the entirely new perspective it foisted on his life. I had given him an image of Bertha Sommer's life which he had never imagined. He had thought of every other permutation of her life. He had wished her well as she drifted out of his memory.

'Did she ever talk about the shooting?' he asked.

'She mentioned something.'

'She wasn't able to forget it,' he said. Dreaming again. It was as though he was suddenly back in the past. 'That's what the heavy secret was. She couldn't forget. Maybe if we were still together, she might have got over it. I couldn't get it out of my head, either. I suppose we were afraid there would be a trial, an investigation. There was no need for any of that. It was a big mistake. All of it.'

He talked for a long time. Explained everything. The light faded outside. Another feeble /wintry evening. Kitchen windows began to steam up everywhere in Nuremberg. TVs came on. Cartoons. News. Football results. People all over Germany sealed into their own luck.

'It was a mistake,' he said. 'They were different times. Everybody had to get away with their own lives. Everybody had a duty to themselves. Every woman has a duty to be a woman. People like Bertha had a duty to survive. There was nothing for her to regret. She had nothing to hide. She was nothing but honesty.'

The phone rang. It looked as though Kern was going to ignore it. I asked if I should answer it for him. It was Maria. I called her Frau Jazinski, giving her the proper respect. She said she was coming over again to make an evening meal. I was welcome to stay and have something to eat.

There was a slight panic. There was a lot that Franz Kern and I had not yet discussed. He was still determined to keep his daughter out of all this.

'There is no point in her asking me endless questions at this stage. It would turn the place into a war tribunal.'

'How much does she know?' I asked.

'Nothing.'

I looked at him with some obvious surprise.

'She knows about Laun. She knows that I fled from the Russians. That I saved a girl's life. That I was involved in a skirmish with partisans and rescued a girl from certain death. My daughter is proud of me. As proud as you can be in this country . . .

'But she knows nothing about Bertha. She doesn't know that I loved Bertha. That I would have gone anywhere with her . . . That I was mad about her . . .

'And I never told anyone that I killed two men long after the war was over. Well, maybe it was the twilight of the war. Maybe the war wasn't over. Maybe it's still not over.'

Kern stood up. He grimaced and said he had some pain in his leg that was 'tormenting him. He made a remark about being told by people that pain and pleasure were the same thing. He wasn't convinced. He smiled and walked over to an antique bureau, unlocked a small, carved door and searched around for something. He held his stick pinned against the bureau with his knee.

'I've never forgotten your mother,' he said.

He came over and handed me a locket.

'This used to belong to her. I think you should have it now. She gave it to me before she disappeared. I never saw her again. I had no idea where she went.'

I looked at the locket for a while. Kern switched on a low table lamp so that I could see better.

'She got it in France, I think.' Then he stood looking out through the window into the dark, beyond the reflection of the interior, the table lamp, the furniture of his own living-room, as though he could actually see something out there, as though he could see right back to the Fichtel mountains, to the lake, and the woods.

I handed the locket back towards him but he refused to take it back.

'No. I want you to have it. I am glad you came. I wouldn't like to have given it to anyone else.'

He stood looking out of the window or at the reflection of the room. I stood beside him. It was as though the two of us were looking at each other in a mirror.

'Am I German or American? Or Polish?' I asked, suddenly.

I regretted asking this almost as soon as I had said it.

'You don't have to answer if you don't want to. I understand.'

'I couldn't answer that,' he said, turning around. 'I wouldn't know. But it feels like talking to a son.'

I could see that it was all beginning to upset him. His eyes had become watery. I could see how old he was now. He

159

reached out his arm to place it around my shoulder and I helped him back to his chair.

'Now tell me about Vermont,' he said.

He wanted to know everything. Every small detail. He asked me to tell him about myself, what I was doing. Where I was living. He saw that I was still holding the locket in my hand and told me to put it away before his daughter came back.

There were further pauses as he took the whole picture of Bertha Sommer's life into his memory. It was as though her life had been lived out in an hour, while we were talking. He had spent his whole life searching for her in his imagination. He had settled for vague explanations, imaginary versions of her life which he could live with. It was as though she had suddenly come back to him. He would have to change his whole life again. He had to adjust his past; everything.

'You look like her,' he said again, staring at me.

42

Germany was spectacular. The fields shone with new crops. The sun had become hotter and lifted the smells of the farms along the way. New-born calves leaped around their mothers on the green pastures.

After Bayreuth, Bertha and Franz cycled into a flatter land-scape, where the avenues and roads were alive with flies and bees and midges. Whenever they stopped, which was quite fre-quently, they often had to keep beating them off with their hands. Once again, they had slowed down the pace of their journey.

In the villages, they were given small portions of food to help them on. Mostly bread. They bartered some of their jam. There was never enough because of the shortages everywhere. They were always hungry. Bertha had lost weight. But she was brown and glowing from the sun.

They cycled for days. The more they cycled, the more the war and what happened to them in the Fichtel mountains receded into the past. They could even talk about it, occasionally, because talking helps you to forget, they thought. Occasionally, there was regret. Bertha thought it was wrong to have left the bodies uncovered in the woods. Maybe they should have been buried. Maybe somebody should have said a prayer over them. But she agreed that it was impossible, that they had had to leave quickly. And Franz kept reminding her that it was no crime, that it was an accident. They would be counted among the millions who died needlessly in the war.

It couldn't be helped. They agreed on that. And every time they agreed not to speak about it ever again. Let's not talk about that any more. It's over.

The weather grew warmer all the time, and balmy. Sometimes it was oppressive. Sometimes Bertha's navy dress clung to her after the cycling. She wished she could wash or bathe some-where. Her soap had almost run out. Only a thin wafer of it was left, the size of a host. There wasn't a bar of soap to be found in the whole of Germany, she thought. They stayed out most nights. Once or twice, they were put up and allowed to sleep on the floor in the villages or the farm-houses along the way.

They were coming closer to Nuremberg all the time. There was no hurry now. Some of the days were so hot and clammy that it made travelling impossible. Without much food, proper sleep or any opportunity to wash, it was difficult to move much. And everywhere the air was still and thick. The country smells of cattle and grass and pigs and woodsmoke slowed things down even further. One morning a wind came up, a wonderful breeze swept across the fields, down from the Fichtel mountains which they had left far behind them.

They should have known. It was followed by a very sudden thunderstorm which caught them both out in the open, in the middle of Germany, without a house in sight, or even a tree to shelter under. They got soaked. They stopped along the road and Bertha made some attempts to cover them both with her russet coat. But they were already soaked. And the rain was ruthless.

It was a cool rain. They gave in to it and enjoyed the soaking. Bertha laughed. She hadn't felt rain like this since she was a child. What they wanted to avoid became a luxury. Within twenty minutes, the sun was out again, raising the steam from the roads, drying everything almost as quickly as it had got wet.

They walked down a lane and stopped at a field, high with corn. Bertha had to change, or dry her clothes. She was left with no choice but to take her dress off to dry it. All her other dresses were too tight for cycling. She berated the fashion that made clothes impossible for walking and moving about in. But then, she was determined to keep her good dresses intact.

Franz found a secluded spot and flattened a square of young corn where Bertha could sit for a while under the sun and get dry. She sat in her underwear, in a white slip, her only good one left. The sun was so strong that her hair was dry within minutes; so dry that she had to loosen strands that had gone rigid.

She felt the luxury of taking off her shoes, feeling the ribbed stems of corn under the soles of her feet. It was great to sit on anything other than a saddle. By now she hated cycling. She sat with her knees up, her hands holding her slip up over her knees. From where Franz stood, the sun illuminated her thighs through the slip; he tried not to look, keeping his eyes towards the road, to make sure nobody came. But the land was empty.

'Franz,' she called.

He turned, holding his hand up to shield his eyes from the sun. She was holding something towards him.

'I want you to have this, Franz. For saving my life.'

'Oh no. I couldn't take that from you.'

'No, you must. I insist. I want you to have it. I want you to carry it with you. I want you to know how grateful I am to you, no matter what happens to us now.'

'But nothing will happen to us now.'

'I insist. I want you to keep this.'

He took it. It would have offended her if he hadn't. He sat beside her, thanked her, said there was nothing to thank him for because he would have done anything for her. She told him to put it away safely into his pocket and never to lose it. It was valuable. How much was impossible to say. The *Reichmark* was worth nothing. She said it was probably worth thousands of dollars. She was joking. They began to think in dollars as they kissed.

They kissed and laughed. After a while, Bertha sat up for a moment to tell Franz something serious.

'I want you to know, Franz, that you were the only man with me, ever.'

She hesitated. She looked at the ground, at her feet on the straw stems of the corn.

'I mean. There was nobody else . . .'

She had difficulty saying what she meant to say.

'Franz,' she said, gathering courage, 'what I meant to say was

163

that you are the only man who has been inside me. Those men in the forest, they didn't succeed. You rescued me in time.'

Bertha blushed and looked away. Franz drew her towards him.

'Bertha, don't think about it. Bertha, *mein Schatz*. Let's not say any more about it.'

Bertha pushed him over. He lay on his back and pulled her down on top of him. It was easy to forget with Franz. He dissolved memories, evaporated them like the rain-water on the roads.

'I'm not cycling another metre today,' she said. 'I refuse. I'm on strike.'

Bertha giggled. She felt it was time to laugh again, and began to tickle him. She kept thinking what all this must look like from above. She had an aerial view of herself in the corner of a rectangular field, her blue pleated dress thrown over a hedge with arms stretched out like a sunbather. Her own bottom in the air, covered only by Franz's strong, bronzed hands on her white skin.

She was afraid of nothing.

43

It was Jürgen who called me for the funeral. He spoke very evenly as usual; his doctor's voice.

'I thought you would like to know,' he said. 'Alexander died yesterday evening. Anke and I would like it very much if you could come to the funeral.'

'Of course,' I said. 'I'm very sorry to hear it.'

I didn't ask him any questions. I felt it wasn't appropriate over the phone or at that time, unless Jürgen volunteered. He didn't. I assumed he had gone through with his plan and was protecting me from any involvement.

'He died peacefully?' I asked.

'Yes,' Jürgen answered briefly. It came like a full admission. He would say no more. He gave me the time of the funeral and said he looked forward to seeing me.

I was on the Intercity once more, early in the morning, looking like a businessman. I don't know what it is about funerals that is like a business. What I felt about Alexander was not the tragedy of his death, but his release from his pain. Maybe I thought of death as something like a trophy. I was sad for Anke, and sad for Jürgen. They were left with nothing.

I don't know why I attract so many businessmen on these train journeys. On my way to Münster for the funeral, I got talking to another man in a suit, who might equally have been going to a funeral had he not told me he was going to a meeting in Osnabrück. He was in cosmetics. They were branching into the East in a big way. That was what his meeting was going to be about. He had been chosen to take on the East.

'It's wonderful, isn't it. The Berlin Wall down. German unity. All this freedom. Europe is a new world.'

'Yes,' I said. I could hardly say otherwise, on the Intercity.

'It's wonderful,' he kept saying. Telling me where his company was planning its strategy. He was open about his joy. He went further, perhaps, than he should have gone, telling me trade secrets, things you would say only to a friend or a complete stranger. I could have been a commercial spy. The great new spy stories are all going to shift from political espionage into commercial espionage. New le Carrés. Maybe the famous Glienecke Bridge in Berlin will now be used to swap managers, planners or chemical engineers under cover of darkness.

This businessman was so enthusiastic, he was almost drunk on progress. He talked about Berlin with great excitement.

'Imagine,' he said. 'All the people who own property beside the Wall. Some of the worst districts up to now. And overnight . . . they became millionaires. And those people in the East, living in wooden houses along the outer border of West Berlin, their wooden shacks become priceless overnight, holiday homes. God knows what.'

He invited me for coffee in the *Speisewagen*, where we sat at the table opposite each other. The white tablecloth bore the Intercity mark. Then he let me in on a personal secret. He wasn't going to stay with his firm. He was going to make it on his own. It was the big chance.

'Oh no. I'm not going to let it go by,' he said. 'My place is going to be Prague. Prague is the big one. Wait till you see.'

He drew back. He wasn't going to tell me what his scheme was. What exact business he had in mind. But he said he had already been there five times since the Velvet Revolution. He was learning Czech like a maniac. He was waiting for the right moment.

Münster was pouring rain. I got a taxi and remembered how Anke said it was one of the rainiest towns in Germany. I went straight to the church. I was there to see Anke arriving with Jürgen, surrounded by relatives. I had met Anke's mother before and I also recognized Jürgen's parents. Anke seemed calm, less solemn than I had imagined, though she wore a black dress. Must have bought it for the day. I'd never seen it before.

166

The size of the small coffin got to everyone. People remarked on it with tragic expressions. I saw Anke and Jürgen both crying together; he was supporting her. It was the way I imagined Anke; as though she was only completely perfect when she was crying. It seemed as though she was crying for everyone.

I could think of nothing but Alexander. I thought about his fringe, about his laugh, the way he enjoyed the simplest of things like the sound of a spoon ringing in a cup. I thought of the time he ran into the living-room with the plunger; Jürgen first wanted to take it off him, then he let him have it, then he helped him stick it to the window and the three of us sat back and laughed helplessly at it.

Outside the church, the weather was very bad. The rain had let up a little, but it was windy and cold. There was no time to stand around for extended condolences after the service. Anke came over to me briefly and said, 'Thank you for coming.' I understood. What else could she say? But I've never felt as distanced from anyone as I did from Anke just then. I tried to say something back. What do you say? I found nothing. And anyhow, she was quickly whisked away into the black limousine. There were too many limousines. It looked like there was one for each mourner, almost.

I was offered a lift with one of the many relatives. Jürgen's uncle, as it turned out. The car I got into was packed. The occupants spoke about Anke. They said she was a courageous woman. They kept saying how much they admired the couple for what they had done. They were not afraid of life. Everyone hoped life would treat them better now. There was an endless stream of cars; some relatives, most of them Jürgen's patients or associates. The practice was closed for the day. Large notices were placed in the papers marking the death of their son.

I almost envied Jürgen and Anke sitting in the first car together, all alone, like a black wedding. This was Anke's real wedding, I thought. A wedding of tears.

The cortège moved slowly past their house, carrying Alexander for the last time past his home, past his toys, his story books, his bed, his special mug, his spinning top. It seemed strange to be travelling so slowly on that street; some of the neighbours coming out on to the pavement to bless themselves and lower their heads in respect. It felt ridiculous: I could have walked faster. The pace of a funeral. There are some things you can't rush. Sometimes you are dragged past a set of images or symbols so slowly, you feel trapped. Unable to move.

At the crematorium, there was another scramble for shelter. It was lashing. Anke was rushed inside, somebody protecting her from the rain with a jacket. Another man made a hood out of his own jacket. I saw a woman holding a handbag up over her head. Everywhere, logistical conversations broke out; how to get from the car to the door of the crematorium in the fastest time. Anke was wet anyway. Her short hair was marked with blobs of rain. Her skin was pale. Her lips were red.

Alexander disappeared. It was very quiet. Somehow it went faster than I expected. Afterwards, I got to speak to Jürgen. He put his arm around me and said, 'I'm glad you came. Above all people, I'm glad you could make it.'

I had another word with Anke too. She put her arms around me for a moment. It was a funeral hug. She seemed happier than I expected. It was as though all the mourners were desperately trying to keep her from being happy ever again. Anke said she was happy that I came. It made her feel good.

'I'll miss you,' she said. 'I'll write to you. I'll tell you everything.'

Before I was able to say a word, she was taken away. She was introduced to other relatives, more distant relatives. Everybody wanted to say a few words to the bereaved mother. Everybody wanted to belong to such a beautiful death, such a beautiful sad mother. Such remarkable sadness. She looked spectacular in grief.

This was Anke's real wedding. This was where I would have to say goodbye.

44

Nothing could have prepared Bertha and Franz for Nuremberg. They could see that the city had been levelled by the last months of the war. It was a wrecked city. The spires and the outline of buildings, which would have been familiar to Franz even from that distance, were razed. The character of Nuremberg had disappeared.

The roads leading to Nuremberg were busier, lined with people on the move. On the outskirts, they came to an encampment of American troops where everybody was being stopped at a roadblock. Bertha saw the Stars and Stripes flying over the camp and thought in a way that she was already in America. For her, as for most of the people returning home, they were friendly colours. The colours of success and liberty. But Franz was certain there would be questions. They would have to identify themselves and say where they had come from.

'Say nothing,' he said to Bertha. 'Whatever you do, say nothing about the shooting. Say nothing at all about that incident.'

They put together a hasty alibi before they merged with the traffic going towards the checkpoint. It was clear that Franz had belonged to the Wehrmacht. He still wore the boots. He wasn't denying anything.

They became separated. Bertha was taken into one barracks while Franz was taken in another direction. 'Say nothing,' she kept repeating to herself. They were made to answer for themselves. Names, addresses, war records. Each of them had to fill in a questionnaire, a list of National Socialist organizations to which they may have belonged. She had belonged to only one of them, the last on the sheet, an insignificant NS trade union which was compulsory for those employed in the state service.

It felt like the final judgement day, Bertha thought to herself. She was nervous. Nervous, because for the first time in her life she could not be entirely honest. She was hiding something. It robbed her of confidence, even though she liked the Americans.

The officer behind the desk asked her where they had disarmed. She said, 'Eger.' There were no more questions and she was allowed to travel on. She found the Americans very good-natured and humorous. They wished her good luck. She tried out a number of English phrases which she had learned at school.

She had to wait a while until they also released Franz Kern. He had been asked where they got the bicycles. And what took them so long in getting back from Eger. But once his identity had been verified, he was allowed to move on. They were cleared.

From then on, Bertha and Franz were struck by the sight of the wrecked city ahead of them. Neither of them wanted to go any further. They wanted to head out, back into the country. They sat down at the side of the road and talked. Franz wanted to turn around and head straight for Hamburg.

'It will be a lot simpler,' he said. 'Then we won't have to explain. And we won't have to see what happened here. We won't get involved.'

He was afraid of what lay in front of him. He was afraid to look for his wife or his mother.

'But you must go and talk to them,' Bertha said. 'It is terribly unfair if you don't. You can't let them suffer, not knowing where you are. You're here now, you have to see them.'

They cycled a little, as far as the streets were clear. They dismounted when they came into streets where the piles of rubble on both sides had left only a narrow path in the middle. Few of the houses still had their roofs on. Many of the three- or four-storey houses were reduced to the height of garden walls. Some of the streets were impassable, with large craters. Everywhere, people were scrambling over the ruins, searching for possessions or relatives.

Franz became more worried as he moved on. He also became more eager. They hurried through the torn city to get to the street where he had lived with his wife Monica and his mother.

The house was gone completely. So were the houses next door on either side. He made his way across the mound of bricks, unable to believe that this was once the place where he lived since he was a child, and since he got married. There was nothing left. He went to the house of his wife's mother and found it had been burned out. None of the floorboards were left. It was black. He assumed the worst and once again felt like leaving Nuremberg for ever.

But Bertha insisted that he had to be sure. He had to look and make inquiries. They asked some of the people in the street what had happened and where all the people had gone to. Some of them were in the country. Many of them had died during the bombing. Some of the survivors were sheltering in camps on the outskirts of the city.

Bertha and Franz found a place to stay for the night. It was a place on the floor in a building among all the ruins which had been left totally intact. The house was packed with people and families. They slept in a room with twenty others. Franz was worried about the bicycles, which they had to leave along the stairs of the cellar where other families were asleep. They slept soundly under Bertha's coat.

The following morning they found the bicycles where they had left them and went through the streets once more making inquiries. They went back to the street where Franz had lived, hoping that if Monica was alive, she would come back there too. Eventually, Franz met a neighbour who told him where his wife was staying.

Bertha and Franz talked about what they would say to her. He would give her the news slowly. She would realize that it was over. Monica could start a new life on her own.

They hurried over there. Both of them had become excited at the news of finding her alive. At the door of an old apartment block which was half standing, up to the second floor, they asked one of the older children standing around for Monica Kern. It was the first time it really dawned on Bertha that they had been looking for his wife. It was when he announced her name that she stood back and prepared herself for the reality.

Monica came running through the courtyard. She was crying long before she reached Franz. She ran to him and threw her arms around him. She couldn't control the shock of her joy. She held on to him and repeated his name. Children who had been playing around in the courtyard all congregated shyly in the arch to watch, some of them perhaps wishing it was their own father.

Monica's tears were streaming. She stood back and looked at Franz. She pulled up her apron and wiped her tears so that she could see him properly.

'I can't believe it,' she said, clapping her hands together. 'They told me that a man was looking for me at the door. Franz, Franz, Franz . . . Thank God you're back.'

She embraced him again. Franz turned her gently towards Bertha and introduced her.

'Monica, this is Bertha Sommer who was with us in Laun. We came back on the bikes together.'

Monica stepped towards Bertha and embraced her.

'Thank you for bringing Franz back to us. I am so grateful. I still can't believe it. We've heard nothing for weeks, months now.' She pulled them both by the arms. 'Now, come on in. I'm sure you're both starving. And exhausted. You've come a long way.'

She told one the older boys in the yard to take in the bicycles and put them in the cellar. Then she led Bertha and Franz up the stairs to a small room. There were four other women in the room. Monica's mother, who was very old now. Another elderly aunt and two younger women, one of them married, as Monica explained, and still waiting for her husband. They had all been staying together in the one room.

'Our house is gone now,' Monica said quietly. 'Luckily, your mother got away to the country before the bombing started.'

'I know, I heard from the neighbours.'

Monica had an extraordinary enthusiasm and ability to turn the mood. Everyone had enthusiasm. It was all that was left. She couldn't stop herself looking at Franz and smiling.

'What you must have gone through,' she said. 'You must tell me everything. But first of all, you must have a good meal. We have a lovely lentil *Eintopf* all ready for you . . .

'Bertha, do you wish to use the bathroom first? We still have a tiny piece of soap. You can have it.'

Monica showed Bertha to the bathroom on the landing. The entire plaster had come down from the ceiling. Bertha could look up at the evening sky and at the side wall of the building, which showed the remains of wallpaper and former homes. The bathroom had been arranged very neatly. There were flowers beside the bath. And towels hanging from a rail. The water had been brought up in buckets and basins, collected that way from the rain.

Bertha washed slowly. It was a deep luxury. Even the feeling of being inside a house with a private bathroom gave her a sense of home. She knew there were so many small things to enjoy in this world, now that the war was over. Water made her happy. She washed her feet.

Bertha wondered when Franz was going to give Monica the news of their intentions to go to America. Perhaps he would just leave a note. Perhaps he was already telling her now.

At dinner, they all sat around the table while Monica served the lentil stew. All in all there were eleven at the table. Five women, including Monica's mother and aunt, along with four young children belonging to the other women, Frieda and Caroline. Occasionally, there were great bursts of conversation. At other times, everybody was quiet, all staring at Franz. He was the only man they had seen in weeks. They all spooned the pale stew, young and old, unable to take their eyes off Franz Kern.

At one stage, Monica began to cry again.

'I still can't believe it,' she said, wiping her eyes with her apron again.

Her mother held her arm and said, 'We're all very happy for you, my dear.'

They asked Bertha where she came from. And Bertha told them about her home town of Kempen.

'Do they know you're coming back?' Monica's mother asked.

'No, not yet,' Bertha answered. And suddenly, amidst this strange extended family in Nuremberg, she had a fierce longing to be with her own family. She could see their joy when she walked in the door. Bertha stared down at her soup, imagining the faces of her mother and her sisters.

'How will you get home from here?' Monica asked.

'I don't know really,' Bertha said. She looked at Franz for support. If ever there was a moment to speak up, this was it. But Franz postponed it again.

The chance was lost.

'Ach, there will be lots of traffic heading in that direction towards Frankfurt,' Monica's mother said. 'What do you think, Franz?'

He said he wouldn't know. The chance was lost again.

The children were put to bed. They went to sleep on the floor while the adults sat at the table and talked. Franz had said nothing yet. Perhaps he was leaving it till the next day. Perhaps it seemed too cruel. At times, Bertha thought of bringing up the subject of herself and Franz. But there were too many people in the room.

They all had to sleep on the floor. There was hardly room for them all. As expected, Franz slept by the cooker, beside Monica. Bertha was given a place by the door, where she slept alone under her coat, looking up at the ceiling, at the patches where the plaster had fallen off and all the cracks where the plaster was ready to give. She was exhausted. But she couldn't sleep. She had a constant feeling that the plaster above her was about to fall.

It was also the feeling that she was indoors. After so many days out in the open, sleeping under the stars, she felt claustrophobic. Her sense of smell had heightened, too, which added to her confined feeling. Most of all, she missed Franz. He was still so close to her, she recognized his breathing among the others.

She stayed awake all night, and slowly began to realize how far away he really was. Some time before dawn she decided it was too cruel to take him away again. She got up and gathered her things quietly and disappeared. The only thing that kept her from crying was the sound of her own footsteps and the thought of her own home in Kempen.

If Franz still wanted to come to America, he would know where to find her.

At 6 o'clock, Bertha Sommer stood on the main road from Nuremberg to Frankfurt. There were many vehicles on the road already at that time of the morning. Most of them were full. Then came a convoy of American trucks and one of them stopped to pick her up.

She sat in the back of the truck with the soldiers. At first she was quiet. She knew she was ready to burst into tears any minute. But then the soldiers began to ask her questions in English and she had to concentrate. She made use of what phrases she knew to explain that she was going as far as Kempen, Niederrhein. She had to cross the Rhine, she told them awkwardly, with the aid of hand movements.

Later, one of the soldiers asked her if she could sing 'Lili Marlene'. She said yes, but it was far too early in the day. They persisted. Eventually she did sing it for them. They clapped and cheered. Some of them offered her cigarettes. Some of them offered chewing gum. She didn't take either. Then they asked for another song, and she sang a song which was later made famous by Elvis Presley under the title 'Wooden Heart'.

> *Muss i denn, muss i denn, zum Städtele 'naus,*
> *Städtele 'naus, und du mein Schatz bleibst hier?*